THE
WINDSOR
KNOT

THE
WINDSOR
KNOT

An Elizabeth MacPherson Mystery

◆

SHARYN McCRUMB

BALLANTINE BOOKS
NEW YORK

Text design by Beth Tondreau Design / Mary A. Wirth

Manufactured in the United States of America

Quality Printing and Binding by:
THE MAPLE-VAIL BOOK MANUFACTURING GROUP
Pine Camp Drive
Binghamton, N.Y. 13902 U.S.A.

ISBN 0-345-36583-6

FOR ROY AND JEAN FAULKNER,
ACCESSORIES BEFORE THE FACT

CHAPTER

I

TWO-THIRDS OF THE people on the list would have
to be eliminated and the decision rested with Adam
McIver, aged twenty-nine, a minor civil servant in Her
Majesty's government.

McIver, late of Fettes College and the University
of Edinburgh, stared wearily at the list of names on
the otherwise empty expanse of mahogany in front of
him. On the other side of the table, Sir Spencer Duff-
Binning (Cambridge, late Pleistocene) was sprawled

in his black leather captain's chair, his nose buried in the current issue of *The Sun* (which he kept tucked inside a copy of the more respectable newspaper, *The Scotsman*). Although he was the project director, and in theory even more responsible for the decision than Adam, he was apparently unconcerned with the grave task that lay before them. The decision had to be made at once, and Sir Spencer Duff-Binning (known as the Old Duffer only after his departure from the building) did not seem inclined to be helpful.

Twice now Adam had cleared his throat meaningfully and remarked, "Well, better get on with it!" The only response from the portly figure behind the newspaper was a grunt and a rustle of pages. Adam glanced at his watch, and again at the paperwork in front of him. He had just cleared his throat for the third time, intending to make a more direct suggestion for getting to work, but his introductory utterance was drowned out by the clatter of a metal cart and the call of "Tea time!" shouted in brassy Glaswegian from the doorway. Adam sighed and summoned a pale smile for Mrs. Drury, the tea lady, who was maneuvering her cart into the room as if she were docking a destroyer.

Another distraction.

Sir Spencer looked up from his newspaper with a happy smile and waved her over. "Got any chocolate Bath Oliver biscuits today, Mrs. D.?"

Adam inspected the cake selection without favor. "Just tea, thanks."

While Sir Spencer and Mrs. Drury nattered on about their respective gardens, name-dropping flowers at a dizzying rate, Adam accepted his cup of tea and returned his attention to the list. When he had chosen a career in the civil service, he had been fully prepared to accept the gravest responsibilities in carrying out his country's affairs of state. Just now, though, he was finding it a bit difficult. In some ways officialdom in Edinburgh's Old St. Andrews House was much as he had imagined it from childhood. He looked around the oak-paneled room, with its shelves of gilt-titled books, black marble fireplace, and the blue government-issue Wilton carpet. It looked like a room in which major policy decisions ought to be made. Except in wartime. Where did the major historic events take place then?

"In tents, I suppose," said Adam, thinking aloud.

Sir Spencer stopped stirring his tea and looked up. "What's that?"

"Nothing, sir. Just wondering where the country's great decisions are made."

"In tents, you said? Absolutely. Quite a lot of policy decisions are made in tents. Except in wartime, of course. It's castles, then. Or fortified basements. But nowadays, tents are the usual thing. Diplomats crowd under them at state funerals, when they get together to do a little bargaining between the psalms, so to speak. Rally round the punch bowl at garden parties. Ascot. That sort of thing."

"Railway carriages, too," said Adam, still thinking of history.

"Oh, *that*," said Sir Spencer in chilling tones. "Well, it guaranteed the succession, but I'd hardly call that particular episode a *policy decision*."

"Ending World War I not a policy decision?" said Adam. "I was thinking of the Armistice. It was signed in a railway carriage in France, wasn't it?"

"Oh, *that*. Indeed," said the old man, more red-faced than usual. "I thought you were referring to an incident in the courtship of the present Prince of Wales."

Blushing, Adam returned to the subject of his immediate concern. "I'm in a bit of a funk over this list," he admitted. "It's quite a solemn responsibility."

Sir Spencer's attention strayed back to page three of his newspaper. "Well, just make a little cross beside the names that you select," he said. "I'll back you up. There'll be no whining from the rest, you know. They're British, aren't they?"

"Well . . . actually, I believe we have to include fifty Americans."

"Yes, but you don't have to *choose* them. Their ambassador will do that. Get on with it. Who have you got so far?"

"Director-general of the Forestry Commission, the Regius Keeper of the Royal Botanic Gardens, the chairmen of the Bank of Scotland and the Royal Bank of Scotland, the lord provost of Edinburgh . . ."

Sir Spencer was not impressed. "Those are the easy ones," he said with a smirk.

Adam nodded in agreement. "I know. It's the others that I feel for. Those who have only one chance."

Mrs. Drury had been making a great show of attending to the tea service so as not to be thought eavesdropping, but this last declaration had rendered all pretense of disinterest useless. "Excuse me, I'm sure," she said, straining for a peek at the document. "But about your list there—oughtn't you to put in a lot of doctors and nurses?"

Adam frowned. "Well, we have a couple of surgeons, of course, and two veterinary surgeons, but . . . nurses?"

The tea lady nodded. "It seems to me that medical folk—and firemen, now that I think of it—are the sort of people that ought to have first place in the fallout shelters. Not bankers!" She sniffed at the impracticality of bureaucrats.

Adam was at sea. "I'm sorry," he stammered. *"Fallout shelters?"*

Mrs. Drury pointed to his list. "Aye. You've been talking about your grave responsibility of deciding who should be included. What else could it be?"

"Something even more momentous," said Sir Spencer solemnly. "We are determining who shall be asked to the Queen's garden party in Edinburgh."

Mrs. Drury shook her head. "Fallout shelters is easier. Them that gets left out won't be around to argue with you." With that pronouncement, she pushed the tea cart toward the door, leaving them to their task.

Several minutes later Adam McIver stopped in mid-check mark as he noticed the next name on the list. "Hel-lo!" he cried. "Cameron Dawson! I was in school with him."

Sir Spencer grunted. "What's he down for?"

Adam consulted the biographical sheet. "It says here that he's a marine biologist. Doctorate from Edinburgh. Areas of specialization something-something; papers in—oh, here we go. Remember when we had that epidemic among seals in the North Sea? We were afraid that they were all dying of pollution."

"Vaguely," said Sir Spencer, who preferred horses to seals.

"It turned out that they had distemper. One of them had been bitten by a dog on a beach somewhere. Apparently, Cameron Dawson was one of the people who discovered what disease the seals had, and he worked to control the epidemic. Imagine that! Old Cameron—a medical hero."

"Excellent, McIver. Send him an invitation. You'll

get no end of gratitude from your school chum, and it will go down well with the Duke of Edinburgh, because he's chairman of the World Wild Life Fund." He waved the last Bath Oliver biscuit at McIver. "Send Dr. Dawson to Her Majesty's Scottish garden party. Kill two birds with one *scone*."

◆   ◆   ◆

CAMERON DAWSON frowned at the official-looking ivory envelope, fearing the worst.

His younger brother Ian, who had joined him for tea in the garden, was helping himself to a scone and clotted cream. One of the nice things about being home from college for the summer was that you got to eat decent food again. Ian planned to consume quite a lot of it before the fall term began at Strathclyde.

"Do you want that last ginger biscuit, Cameron?" he asked as he reached for it. When no reply was forthcoming, Ian glanced at his brother, who was still staring at a small ivory envelope. Noting Cameron's stricken expression with interest, he asked, "Anything the matter?"

"Not until now," murmured Cameron, still staring at the letter.

The afternoon had thus far been remarkably pleasant for early June in Edinburgh: it was sunny after only an hour of misting rain, and so warm that one needed only a cotton sweater instead of a wool one. Cameron's yearlong stay as a visiting professor of marine biology at a university in Virginia had considerably reduced his tolerance to the climate of his native Scotland. Today, though, had been quite satisfactory, and having spent his first few days home visiting with family and friends, he had decided to spend the afternoon in the garden so that he could bask in the sunshine while he caught up on accumulated mail and bank statements and other bits of paperwork that had arrived too recently to be forwarded to him in America. He had been enjoying colors of the well-tended garden, with its well-pruned privet hedge, its herbaceous border, and the unfortunate, but nevertheless familiar red-hatted garden gnome, who stood smirking by the forsythia bush. As he leafed through newsletters and back issues of magazines, Cameron savored the aroma of his mother's prize roses. There was nothing to occupy his mind except the prospect of afternoon tea. This peaceful interlude under the rowan tree had been spoiled by the discovery of an official-looking envelope tucked into a pile of advertising circulars from Halford's. Trust Ian to miss an important letter—probably with dire consequences! And the prospect of having to cope with this disaster spoiled his serenity just as the tea arrived.

"What is it, then? Inland Revenue?" asked Ian,

dumping sugar into his teacup. "Getting you for all that money you made in the States?"

"Shut up, Insect," murmured Cameron. "You should have forwarded this to me, or else opened it and phoned me about it. It's rather important looking. Addressed to *Dr*. Cameron Dawson."

"Ye-ess," said Ian gravely. "That *is* you, is it not? Or have you an evil twin that I am unacquainted with? I don't think I could stand the thought of another sibling at this late date."

Cameron opened the envelope and took out a card-sized invitation, printed in graceful script. He read it twice. "I was afraid of this." He sighed, handing the letter to his brother.

Ian's eyes widened at the sight of the royal coat of arms. "It's from—" He scanned the card, muttering an occasional word aloud. "Well, imagine that! An invitation to the Royal Garden Party! Did someone from Fettes put you up for this? I sense an Old School Tie dangling over all this."

"Adam McIver, I expect. He was always a proper little prat, quite intent on government service. The bugger!"

"Steady on, Cameron. It's only a tea party. You act as if you'd been commissioned in the Light Brigade."

"Yes, Ian, but you don't comprehend the possibilities for trouble here. You see, they've just invited *me*. And you know what a maniac Elizabeth is about the Queen. She's always reading royal biographies and asking me daft questions about the latest palace scandal, as if I'd know anything about it. She may even have been named for the sovereign, for all I know." Cameron sighed. "I suppose that I could ring up the committee and ask them to invite Elizabeth as well."

"Not a hope," said Ian. "No guests except spouses and unmarried daughters. You haven't any of *those*, I trust?" he added mischievously.

"Elizabeth and I are engaged. . . ."

"I don't believe fiancées are permitted to attend." Ian chuckled. "There's many a slip twixt—"

"No, I realize that," snapped Cameron. "But if I go to the Royal Garden Party without telling her, and somehow Elizabeth finds out that she missed a chance to meet the Queen—"

"Second American Revolution." Ian nodded. "Absolutely. It's curious, isn't it, how starstruck the Yanks are about our royal family? Makes you wonder why they seceded from the empire in the first place."

Cameron looked again at the invitation with Her Majesty's seal for a letterhead. "They do seem to dote on the royals, don't they? People were always asking me if I knew any of them. Elizabeth even has a complete set of royal-family coffee mugs. Only Prince Edward is cracked."

"Yes, I'd heard that," said Ian, grinning wickedly.

"Well, brother dear, what's it going to be? The Queen's tea party or the Boston tea party?"

"I'll just explain to Elizabeth that with the garden party only three weeks away and the wedding planned for *next* summer, we can't possibly manage. They might not include her as an afterthought in any case. . . ."

"Surely Old Adam could put in a word for you," said Ian with a smirk.

"Or perhaps I won't mention it to her at all. After all, how could she find out about this invitation?"

Ian strove to look unconcerned.

Cameron scowled at his younger brother. "You *would*, too, wouldn't you?" he muttered. "Oh, all right! I suppose I'll have to mention it to her before I write my reply—with fulsome apologies for the delay! As for Elizabeth, I'll just reason with her." Cameron clambered out of his lawn chair and started for the house.

"You're going to ring her up now—while the rates are high?"

"Yes," said Cameron. "I want to get it over so I don't brood about it. What time is it in America?" he asked.

Ian called after him, "1776!"

◆　◆　◆

The Lord Chamberlain is
commanded by Her Majesty to invite

Dr. Cameron Dawson

to a Garden Party
at the Palace of Holyroodhouse
on Thursday, 6th July, 1989 from 4 to 6 p.m.

Morning Dress, Uniform or Lounge Suit

CHAPTER

2

AT A PICTURESQUE university in the Blue Ridge of southwest Virginia, the mountain laurel blossomed on shady hillsides and the squirrels scampered under the oaks on the campus quad. All this was wasted on Elizabeth MacPherson, who hunched over a technical journal in the shabby, windowless cubicle reserved for graduate students in forensic anthropology. Her thoughts were far from queen and empire: she was reading about maggots.

The scholarly article detailing the usefulness of insect life in determining time and place of death almost sanitized the subject past the point of gruesomeness. Almost, but not quite. Elizabeth found herself scratching her just-washed hair and brushing imaginary specks of dirt off her khaki skirt. She thought it odd that a mere article would make her squeamish, considering that the examination of corpses was a routine occurrence for her. As a graduate student in forensic anthropology, Elizabeth had become accustomed to all manner of unsavory exhibits. She was inured to gruesome sights, but she had difficulty in controlling her imagination—and that was the trouble with the journal article. Besides, it awakened a childhood memory of her brother putting a fishing worm down her back. She shuddered, remembering the feel of writhing coldness, when she suddenly noticed the word *Scotland* on the page in front of her. With a smile of anticipation, she returned her attention to the text. Maggots were still disgusting, but Scottish maggots seemed more . . . *palatable* was definitely not the word she wanted.

The case description began: *September 29, 1935, about forty miles south of Edinburgh* . . . That would have been in Dumfrieshire, thought Elizabeth, picturing a golden autumn day in the hills of the southern uplands bordering England. A woman was crossing a stone bridge near the town of Moffat when she noticed a bit of color in the stream below. A closer look sent her screaming toward the village: the flotsam in the water was a severed human arm. The Scottish police searched the banks of the stream for days thereafter, eventually finding more than sixty butchered fragments, including two heads, a pelvis, some feet, and a pillowcase full of flesh, all teeming with insect larvae. (At this point in the narrative Elizabeth resolved to stop visualizing the scene.)

The killer had removed all identifying characteristics—eyes, ears, fingertips—from the bodies of the women, but through diligent inquiry the police learned that two women, Isabella Ruxton and her maid Mary Rogerson, were missing from over the border in Lancaster, and that they had been on their way to Edinburgh. Isabella's husband, Dr. Buck Ruxton, insisted that the women were not missing, but they could not be found in Edinburgh, and no one recalled seeing them along the way. Dr. Ruxton, who was known to be notoriously jealous, was charged with murder. But when did the killings occur? The police theorized that the women died on September 19, days after they left Lancaster, which would have provided a good alibi for the doctor.

To test this theory, investigators took maggots from the body parts and sent them to Alexander Mearns at the University of Glasgow. *Not a pretty job, but a useful one*, thought Elizabeth, turning the page. Mearns recognized the larvae of the bluebottle fly and drew up a timetable of their life cycle. Allowing for cold autumn weather to slow the process, Mearns declared that the bodies had been dumped in the ravine near Moffat on September 16, the day after their disappearance, and at the subsequent trial Dr. Ruxton was found guilty of murder.

The Ruxton case marked the first time that maggots had been used to determine time of death. It was one of the historic moments in the annals of her often-unglamorous profession. Elizabeth thought of mentioning this Scottish achievement to her fiancé, but decided that he might not regard it as romantic or complimentary to his homeland. Still, it was interesting. She made a note of the Ruxtons.

The round clock tacked on the cinderblock wall said eight minutes after eleven. If the article became any more graphic, lunch could be postponed indefinitely, which was just as well, she thought, straining to insert her finger into the waistband of her skirt. Perhaps she ought to go in search of more maggot articles for future lunchtime reading. Or she could try *Bride's* magazine. That ought to do it. Where did they find those models? Bangladesh? Elizabeth had resolved not even to daydream about her year-off wedding until she had discernible cheekbones.

It was now June (lion cubs on her World Wild Life calendar), and she contemplated the next twelve months, feeling like someone crouched with her toes on a white line. It was going to be a year of computer screens and boiled rice. (On second thought, that menu reminded her too much of her present reading material. Make that lettuce salads.) In September she would take her orals and then begin writing the dissertation for her doctorate in forensic anthropology. If all went as planned, a svelte (with cheekbones!) Elizabeth would defend before her doctoral committee near the end of the term in May, and then *Dr.* Elizabeth could concentrate on Cameron Dawson, the marine biologist whose picture adorned her desk.

He was spending the summer at home in glorious Scotland, while she was stuck at the university, teaching undergraduate anthropology to disgruntled summer-school hostages in an un-air-conditioned building. *Some people have all the luck,* she thought, frowning at Cameron's picture. And her parents had taken a long-awaited trip to Hawaii, without even a perfunctory expression of regret that she couldn't go along. "Don't call us," they told her. "Not even if one of the relatives dies. We need this vacation."

Elizabeth sighed again. There was some justice: Bill wasn't having a restful summer, either. Her brother was clerking for a law firm in Richmond; she hoped the lawyers were getting their money's worth. At least she would have a break in another week when the spring semester ended, perhaps a week at the beach— Virginia Beach, that is; a poor substitute for Waikiki. And that would be *after* she graded a zillion exams. Then came summer school. A bleak summer of work and dieting. Maybe there was something to be said for being a maggot. They ate all the time, grew enormously fat on purpose, slept it off in a cocoon, and then sprouted wings and burned off all the calories by flying. Not a bad deal. She was considering the possibilities of an insect afterlife when the telephone rang.

"Forensic anthro," she said in her most businesslike tone.

"Good afternoon, Miss Anthro," said an unmistakably Scottish voice.

"Cameron! I was just thinking about you!"

"And why was that?"

Wisely deciding *not* to mention the maggot article, Elizabeth simpered charmingly for a few minutes before it occurred to her to ask, "Why are you calling me in the middle of the day? The rates haven't changed yet, have they?" Such considerations are necessary in a long-distance romance.

"No, no," said Cameron. "I just felt like talking to you. How are things at the university?"

"Dull," said Elizabeth. "I feel like a prisoner in this

Gothic mausoleum. I'd rather be at the beach. How are things with you?"

"Oh, peaceful," said Cameron, who thought it would be unchivalrous to claim to be having a good time when one's fiancée has declared herself miserable. "Miss you, of course."

"I should hope so."

"I do have a bit of good news, actually," said Cameron, endeavoring to sound both casual and innocent. "Thought you might like to hear it. Do you remember that work I did on the project to save the North Sea seals? The country has recognized my work by giving me a bit of an honor. I've been invited to the Royal Garden Party here in Edinburgh."

After a gratifying gasp of awe, Elizabeth said, "What does that mean, exactly? Why do they want to see you?"

"To look after the royal seal!" Cameron laughed— alone—at his little marine-biologist joke, and then proceeded to explain. "Each summer the palace gives two garden parties (one at Buckingham Palace for English notables, and one for Scots at the Palace of Holyroodhouse in Edinburgh) to honor various members of the British public: distinguished civil servants, influential business people, civic officials, and outstanding achievers in the arts and sciences."

"Just the odd thousand or so of the Queen's closest chums," said Elizabeth. "I see."

Cameron saw his chance. "More like eight thousand, I'm afraid. You're right, of course. I doubt if I'll catch more than a glimpse of Her Majesty. Just a dreary function, really."

"I wouldn't miss it for the world," said Elizabeth.

"No, I shan't. Technically one mustn't. After all, it is a royal summons. I'll tell you all about it."

There was a transatlantic silence.

Cameron cleared his throat. "Well, I just thought I'd tell you the news. I know you're rather interested in all the royal goings-on. Thought you'd be pleased for me."

After another frosty interval, Elizabeth said, "You mean you just called me to tell me about the invitation? Don't you have the common decency to invite me along?"

"Well, I *would*, you know, if it were up to me. Really, I would. But one may not bring guests. Except spouses, of course. Fiancées don't count, I'm afraid."

What a coincidence, thought Elizabeth, scowling. *Just as I finish reading an article about Scottish maggots, one of them rings me up.* She wisely refrained from expressing those sentiments aloud.

Cameron, who had interpreted his fiancée's silence as a concession to the force of his arguments, offered another—fatal—bit of logic. "And like an idiot, Ian forgot to send me the letter. So I'm only just finding

◆

out about the invitation now, with the garden party only three weeks away—"

"Three weeks!" cried Elizabeth.

"Yes," said Cameron, more confidently now. "Thursday, the sixth of July. Hardly any time at all, really."

"Three *weeks*! I thought it was *tomorrow*. I can plan a wedding in three weeks! We can go to Edinburgh for the honeymoon! Just imagine getting to meet the Queen on your honeymoon! That ought to show Mary-Stuart Gillespie with her stupid trip to Puerto Vallarta! Oh, Cameron, this is wonderful!"

British reserve was much in evidence on the other end of the line. "I thought your parents were away on vacation—"

"They are. In Hawaii. But Mother is no good at this sort of thing anyway. No, if you really want a society wedding, my aunt Amanda is the only person who can handle it. I'll bet she could even manage it in three weeks. I'm not sure if we could get the invitations *engraved*—raised lettering, I mean—but a good printer can get them done in three days the regular way." Elizabeth stopped short, listening to the voluminous silence from the receiver. "Cameron?"

"Yes. I'm here."

"This is all right with you, isn't it?" she asked softly. "I mean, we were planning the wedding anyway, and I know this is short notice, but *the Queen!*"

Cameron sighed. He had not mistaken her reasonable tone for a willingness to be reasonable. "Well, I hadn't planned on spending my honeymoon in chilly Auld Reekie. Look, how about going to the Bahamas instead? Maybe you can meet Miss Universe."

"Don't be silly. King Farouk was right, you know."

"What? Sorry, bad connection. It sounded like you said *King Farouk*."

"So I did. King Farouk once predicted that in fifty years there would be only five kings in the world: spades, hearts, diamonds, clubs, and the King of England. British royalty is . . . I don't know . . . sort of magical."

"I know." Cameron sighed again. "I had a friend who went to school at Gordonstoun, and he said that the surest way to have it off with a girl was to pretend to be—"

"Cameron!" Elizabeth's tone was ominous.

"All right! All right! Benedict Arnold must be laughing up his sleeve somewhere, you bloody royalist! But if you think you can manage, and if you're set on doing it . . ."

"You don't mind getting married in America?"

"No. I don't anticipate having many guests anyway, since I haven't really kept up with my mates from school. Mother and Ian will come over, of course, and I expect Denny Allan will attend if he can. After all, he knows you from the Banrigh expedition, and besides, he's always wanted to go to Disney World, and this is a perfect excuse to get there. I'll give him a call, and then let you know if he'll be on hand. We can draft him as an usher."

"Good! What about bridesmaids? Any cousins or old girlfriends you'd like to import?"

"No, thank you. You'll have to manage on your own."

"Leave everything to me! Oh, Cameron, thank you! This is going to be so amazing! I'd better get started on the preparations right away. Was there anything else?"

"What? Oh, no. No." Just a small matter of running Adam McIver to earth and squeezing another invitation out of him. Cameron wondered if they'd have to fax over a copy of the marriage license. Which reminded him . . . "Wait! Elizabeth! Don't I have to be in America to apply for the wedding license?"

"I'll see if we can get around that!" his bride-to-be assured him. "My brother is a lawyer, remember?"

Too bad he isn't an archbishop, thought Cameron. "Very well, dear. I'll leave you to it. Let me go and tell the family the good news. Perhaps I ought to call your parents as well. Ask for your hand officially, and all that."

"I have the number of the hotel somewhere here," said Elizabeth, flipping through papers on her desk.

"What time is it in Hawaii, anyhow?" asked Cameron, wondering if the task could be postponed until he got accustomed to the idea himself.

"I don't have a clue," said Elizabeth. "I'm not even sure what *day* it is there. Speaking of days, what date shall we set for the wedding?" She riffled through her calendar. "How about July the first? That's the Saturday before the garden party. Is that date all right with you?"

"Just fine, dear," said Cameron. Ian should have stopped laughing by then. Sighing in resignation, he started to look up the number of Old St. Andrews House, where no doubt Adam McIver was lurking, making trouble for untold numbers of his old schoolmates.

◆ ◆ ◆

Department of Forensic Anthropology

June 12

Dear Bill,

I hope that you have refrained from being a nuisance to your summer employers to the extent that they are willing to release you for a couple of days. Or, conversely, that you have been fired, so that when you slink home in dishonor, you can make yourself useful, because the first part of the summer is going to be very hectic, and we could use all the help we can get.

I am getting married!

Now I know that the drain trap you call a mind has just come up with a number of uncomplimentary explanations for this sudden haste, but you are quite mistaken. For someone who is in training to be an attorney, you certainly do jump to a lot of conclusions.

As a matter of fact, we are getting married on July the first (mark your calendar) so that I can accompany Cameron to the Royal Garden Party in Edinburgh on the sixth! I'm going to make sure this fact gets mentioned in the newspaper article on the wedding.

You are hereby appointed as one of the ushers. So is Cousin Geoffrey, so it is safe to assume that people will be thinking "House of . . ." when contemplating your ushership . . . usherhood. Whatever you call it. I expect the Queen would know; perhaps I shall ask her. Anyhow, I feel safe in allowing the two of you into the wedding party (without being chained together at the ankle, which was my first thought) because the whole affair will be managed by none other than Aunt Amanda, and neither you nor Geoffrey would dare to cross her.

As you may have deduced from this, we are getting married in Chandler Grove, and, yes, Mother and Dad will be back from Hawaii in plenty of time. Meanwhile I am subsisting almost entirely on lettuce. You will be pleased to learn that you will not need a morning coat for the occasion. If I decide to outfit you in kilts, I will let you know.

And, remember, I am the bride, so you have to do as I say.

Love,

Elizabeth

Department of Forensic Anthropology

Dear Bill,

 We are not amused.
 And I advise you not to bother a serious organization like Amnesty International with your frivolous attempts at humor.
 We will see you at the wedding.

Cordially,

Elizabeth

CHAPTER 3

AMANDA CHANDLER replaced the telephone receiver with a soft click and stared off into the distance as if she were still listening to disembodied voices. "What an extraordinary call," she said at last. "The Queen."

Her husband, Dr. Robert Chandler, halted his proofreading of the galleys of his book on colonial medicine and regarded his wife with an expression of concern. He hoped that she wasn't hallucinating again, although the clinic had assured him that Amanda was perfectly fine—as long as she didn't drink. *Had* she been drinking? He didn't think so. Surreptitiously, Dr. Chandler leaned forward in his chair to see if there was a glass on the end table beside her. He didn't see one. He ventured a timid inquiry. "The Queen called you, did she, dear?"

Amanda stared at him over the top of her reading glasses. "Really, Robert! Have you taken leave of your senses? That was Elizabeth on the phone."

Dr. Chandler took a deep breath. "Yes, dear," he said carefully. "I know who the Queen of England is."

"No! I mean, it was our niece Elizabeth. She wants to get married as quickly as possible." Noting his blushing reaction, she added quickly, "There you go again! It's *not* what you think. Do you remember that young man of hers, the one from Scotland?"

"As well as one can remember someone one has never met," Dr. Chandler replied, stealing another glance at his book galleys.

"Cameron Dawson. He's a marine biologist. Well, Elizabeth tells me that he has got invited to some Royal Garden Party that the Queen gives each summer in Edinburgh. They want to get married in time for Elizabeth to go with him. Imagine! An opportunity to meet the Queen."

"That's splendid," he murmured, scribbling a notation in the right margin.

"Yes, I thought so!" Amanda said happily, unaware of her husband's flagging attention. "I had despaired of Elizabeth at one time. She wanted to cut up dead bodies for a living and she didn't seem interested in social proprieties at all, but I see that it was only a phase she had to outgrow. I quite approve of her new self. You'll notice that she knew exactly who to turn to in planning this wedding. The only problem is that Doug and Margaret are in Hawaii for the next two weeks—though they'll be back in time for the ceremony."

"Ceremony?" Dr. Chandler looked up. "Where is the ceremony?"

"Why, here, of course!" With a wave of her hand, she indicated that she meant within the house. "I thought perhaps the front hall for the processional. That oak staircase would look very nice in wedding photographs, and the chandelier provides excellent lighting."

"Er—shouldn't Elizabeth's parents have some say in the matter?"

"She's phoned them, of course, Robert. Margaret has given her the go-ahead. With considerable relief, I would imagine. Naturally, I shall manage the wedding. I am the one with all the social graces in the family. Have I not given a reception for the lieutenant governor of Georgia? All my sister Margaret knows how to do is macramé plant holders and speak bordertown Spanish. Where would *she* hold the wedding—on their *carport?*"

Amanda Chandler's eyes flashed with a sparkle of enthusiasm and her cheeks were flushed. Dr. Chandler noted these details with interest. He had rarely seen his wife so animated since their daughter's death a few years earlier. At that time, Amanda had become depressed and her long-ignored drinking problem had worsened enough for her to be sent away for private treatment. She had been back for some months, and while she had not resumed her drinking, she was still not her old self. Her bright auburn hair showed streaks of the gray she had concealed for years, and she spent long hours in front of the television watching mindless sitcoms. Dr. Chandler had wanted to get more counseling for her, but she had insisted that nothing was the matter.

"I shall have to get my hair done first thing tomorrow," Amanda announced, peering at herself in the gilt mirror above the mantelpiece. "And then I'll start making lists."

Dr. Chandler smiled to himself. The old Amanda was back.

THE CHANDLER HOME was exactly the setting that a bridal magazine might choose for a photo layout. Surrounded by acres of forested hills, the brick Georgian-style mansion was set in a grove of oak trees in a white-fenced enclosure at the center of a rolling meadow. The house had been in the Chandler family for four generations, but its present stateliness was largely ascribable to the efforts of its present owner. Dr. Robert Chandler provided the income to finance the improvements, while his wife Amanda scoured *Southern Living* and various decorator magazines for ideas to refine the simple brick farmhouse. In two decades of relentless renovation, Amanda had demolished the white front porch in favor of a columned portico above the front door, added a one-story family room with sliding glass doors, and replaced the original plaster walls, which showed the age of the house like a wrinkled face. Oak paneling had been installed in the hallways and floral wallpaper adorned every other surface.

The result of these modern amendments was a house that looked like an unspoiled relic of the antebellum South. One could imagine General Sherman halting his mount on a nearby hillside, gazing at the neat brick exterior and well-tended lawn of the Chandler property, and saying, "What a fine house! Let's wipe our feet before we go in *there* to loot!" Actually, the late general (referred to by Southern punsters as

Edifice Wrecks) was never in the vicinity of Chandler Grove, and if he had been, the Chandler farmhouse in its pre-Amanda simplicity would have been beneath his notice.

Now, of course, the house was an object of lust for every realtor in the country. Modern-day Yankees, without the benefit of artillery to negotiate their property deals, would pay millions for the Chandler place. And it wasn't even the biggest or most elaborate house in the county. No, *that* house was across the road from the Chandler mansion, and it *was* for sale, but the realtors weren't sure what to do about it. They couldn't even figure out how to word the advertisement. Realtors shrugged and told each other hopefully that somebody from California would buy it.

◆　◆　◆

"ELIZABETH IS GETTING married *here?*" said Geoffrey Chandler in tones suggesting an outraged Oscar Wilde. "Wouldn't it be more appropriate for her to do it over *there?*" He gestured grandly toward the house across the road.

His brother Charles shrugged in completely unfeigned indifference. "I'm just telling you what Mother said, Geoffrey. Besides, don't you think that getting married in a replica of a Bavarian castle would be tacky?"

"I do indeed," Geoffrey replied. "That is why I was certain she would leap at the opportunity. Can't you just see Elizabeth gliding down the aisle in Lohengrin's swan boat with strains of Wagner in the background?"

Charles shuddered. "Not without a sedative, I can't. Why don't they just get a justice of the peace to marry them in the meadow?"

Geoffrey turned away from the window and regarded his brother with a gleam of malevolent interest. "In the meadow," he repeated, savoring the words. "Flowers in her hair, perhaps? Groom in medieval dress—puffed-sleeve shirt, velvet coat, leather buskins? Processional played on guitar and flute?"

Charles nodded eagerly.

"Write their own vows? Including, perhaps, the odd quotation from García Lorca and *The Prophet?*"

"Yes, exactly!"

Geoffrey smirked. "Just as I thought! Her taste for the gauche is a genetic disorder. And *you* have it, too! How fortunate that I was spared its ravages."

"Really? I should have thought you'd want to wear your cloak and doublet to the ceremony." Charles nodded toward a black velvet costume hanging from a hook on the closet door.

"That is my costume for *Twelfth Night,*" said Geoffrey gravely. "The theatre group is staging it in August. It's quite an appropriate costume for a Shakespearean production; however, I attend all family melodramas in modern dress. Still, this will be an interesting little comedy no matter what anyone wears. When is this blessed event, anyway?"

"On the first of July, according to Mother."

"The first of July of *this* year?" purred Geoffrey. "Speaking of blessed events, perhaps?"

"No. I understand that the haste has something to do with an invitation to meet the Queen."

Geoffrey strove to look unimpressed. "This will be an occasion of note, then," he murmured. "Perhaps we should both brush up on wedding etiquette, Charles."

Charles's lips tightened. "I am a scientist," he announced grandly. "My concerns are above matters of social conventions. I am unworldly."

"You are unearthly," Geoffrey agreed pleasantly. "Now run along, Charles. I must go and consult, before Elizabeth concocts an absolutely ghastly public spectacle."

When the door to his room had closed (with more force than is strictly necessary to move a hinged pine board), Geoffrey Chandler walked back to the window and looked across the road at the confection of turrets gleaming in the moonlight. His cousin Alban's architectural flight of fancy had ceased to be merely silly a few years earlier when tragedy had ended plans for another family wedding. Even after years of familiarity had rendered the castle commonplace, Geoffrey could not look at it without a feeling of disquiet.

To him the castle did not conjure up thoughts of Disneyland and Bavarian calendars, but memories of madness and family sorrow. He wished it had been built of spun sugar rather than Georgia granite so that it would melt away in the spring rains. Just as well that Elizabeth was not lumbering her wedding with the emotional baggage of Cousin Alban's castle, he thought. He wondered what she did have in mind.

◆ ◆ ◆

CHARLES CHANDLER stalked off down the hall, trying to mutter the quote about a prophet being without honor in his own country, but he kept getting tangled up over the wording. Literary matters were not within his realm of expertise. The *sentiments* were right, though, he thought with a stab of self-pity. Not only was he without honor in his own family—much of the time he was without ordinary politeness as well. Charles, the earnest and ascetic scientist, felt so out of place in his hearty country family that he took refuge in fantasizing himself as a changeling. He often wondered if Carl Sagan had a son his age who liked touch football and tailgate picnics; and if so, could they arrange to have blood tests?

He wished that it had not been necessary for him to come home again, but his other place of residence, the scientific commune to which he had belonged since college, had been struck by what Charles liked to call Sunnyvale Syndrome, leading to its disbanding and to the relinquishing of the group's long-term lease on the property. The symptoms of Sunnyvale Syndrome included a sudden aversion to orange crates used as furniture and an uncontrollable urge to possess a BMW. In short, Charles's scientific cronies had sold out. One by one, as they passed into their third decade of life, the commune members began to seek out jobs in the computer industry; some of them even applied for teaching positions on the same college campuses they had fled not so long before.

"Face it, Charles," said one deserting yuppie, "even if you are the next Einstein, as long as you stay unaffiliated with a university or corporation, you're never going to get a grant to fund your work, and anyway, the Nobel prizes are rigged politically, so you'd never get one. No bucks, no glory. I mean, what's the point, man?"

Others had warned him about the so-called biological clock of physicists, which was just as ominous in its way as the baby deadline was to women. Charles was past thirty. Virtually all of the great discoveries in the theoretical sciences are made by young minds, his colleagues reminded him. Einstein proposed his special theory of relativity at the age of twenty-six. His fellow physicists Niels Bohr and Werner Heisenberg had won their Nobel prizes by the time they were twenty-eight. Didn't Charles think that it was time to face the obvious; shouldn't he start considering tenure and tax shelters? Stung by their lack of faith in his ability, Charles had retorted that Isaac Newton had been a late bloomer, and that he would show them who was over the hill, but they had given him pitying, disbelieving smiles, and told him to keep the orange crates.

Then he tried to persuade them to spend a few more months testing cold fusion theories. According to reports in the journals, those experiments could be conducted in an ordinary kitchen without expensive equipment; anyone who succeeded in producing cold fusion would become immeasurably rich. Surely it was worth a try? They thought not. With ill-concealed grins they had pleaded prior commitments, so in the end, Charles packed his duffel bag and two orange crates and went home to Chandler Grove. Now he was trying to decide what to do, in case he didn't manage to discover the process of cold fusion. He had nightmares in which Einstein and Alfred Nobel sang "Happy Birthday" to him over a blazing cake with dynamite sticks for candles. He would wake up screaming just as the explosion began. The fact that Charles's sister had spent years in a mental institution did nothing for his peace of mind. Nor did his parents' patronizing attitude toward his work. He thought his parents' hospitality, and his own ability to endure it, might last until the end of the summer.

He welcomed his cousin Elizabeth's forthcoming wedding as a diversion for the rest of the family. Perhaps everyone would become so occupied in meddling in *her* business that they would have less time to bother Charles. The sooner this occurred the better, he thought, and to that end he continued spreading the news about Elizabeth's wedding to all the relatives he could find.

His next stop was a pine-paneled study in the back of the house, decorated with ship models and a framed photograph of Tom Clancy. There William Chandler, affectionately known to his daughters' children as Captain Grandfather, kept himself busy with matters maritime. The old gentleman was seated at his keyhole desk, immersed in the latest edition of *Jane's Fighting Ships*.

"Captain Grandfather!"

The old man looked up, frowning at the interruption. His displeasure with his eldest grandson had been clear for some time now, and he had taken to leaving Coast Guard brochures near Charles's place at the dinner table. "Well, what is it?"

Charles endeavored to look enthusiastic. "Have you heard the news? Elizabeth is getting married!"

The response was a sour look. "What does that mean?" Captain Grandfather demanded. "Tired of graduate school, is she? I wish just *one* of my grandchildren would have the gumption . . ."

Charles stood silently through the tirade, trying to think of something else.

"And who's the groom, pray? I suppose she told him about the inheritance."

A look of wonder illuminated Charles's unexceptional features. He had completely forgotten about the inheritance.

◆　◆　◆

IAN DAWSON WAS still in the garden, reading one of his brother's science magazines when Cameron returned, decidedly paler than when he left.

"What's the matter with you?" asked Ian. "You're looking rather peculiar. More so than usual, I mean."

"I'm getting married," said Cameron.

"Yes, I know."

"I mean *soon*."

Ian burst out laughing. "Let me guess! In time for the Royal Garden Party."

Cameron nodded. "July first."

"Well, congratulations and all that," said Ian, still grinning. "I take it this is voluntary."

"Yes, of course. But sudden."

"Well, I hope it achieves its aim. Did you get up with the Fettes fiend who landed you in this mess?"

"Yes. Fortunately he was in his office. I explained

to him that I was getting married before the event and would like to bring my bride."

"Not telling him how suddenly this wedding had been arranged, I hope?"

"No. He'd have laughed himself into fits."

"And did he promise to get her in?"

"Well, he dithered a bit, but in the end he said he would take care of it. I rather implied that the mistake in omitting her had been *his* fault."

Ian grinned. "You snake!"

"Well it's all his fault, anyway, isn't it?" said Cameron obstinately. "That will teach him."

◆　◆　◆

TARTAN BRIDESMAIDS DRESSES . . . wrote Elizabeth at the top of a sheet labeled WEDDING. "I suppose you can get plaids in something other than wool," she mused aloud. "But if not, let them sweat."

For the remainder of the day, Elizabeth had been of very little use to the anthropology department. After Cameron's phone call, she had tossed the technical journal into a heap of ungraded papers and departed for the library in search of more salient topics for scholarly research. She returned to her office several hours later, staggering under a load of books with titles like *Love and Marriage Among the Royal Family*; *Elizabeth II: A Life*; *Royal Etiquette*; and *Backstairs at*

the Palace: or What the Butler Saw. Now back at her
desk she was rooting happily through pages of Cecil
Beaton photographs of the royal family, making notes
about who was wearing what, and reading pages of
italicized copy describing palace festivities.

"Pages in tiny military uniforms," she said, scribbling furiously. "Wouldn't Captain Grandfather love
that? Not possible, though. There'd be trouble over
whose army got represented. They'd better have kilts.
Clan MacPherson tartan, of course. Cameron can't tell
one plaid from another anyway." After some minutes
of trying to think of any small boys who might qualify
to act as pages at her wedding, Elizabeth was forced
to cross them off her list. Neither she nor Cameron
had any male relatives under twenty.

Her reverie was interrupted by the occupant of the
adjoining cubicle. "Aren't you here awfully late?"
asked graduate student Jake Adair, poking his head
around the partition between their desks. He glanced
at the books spread out in front of her and smiled.
"Switching to a different branch of anthropology?"

Elizabeth shook her head. "No. But thank goodness
you're here. I've been dying to tell somebody. I'm
getting married!" Ignoring Jake's protests that he had
to meet somebody for dinner, Elizabeth proceeded to
tell him all the details of the just-planned wedding.
"And we're going to honeymoon in Scotland, and
meet the Queen at the Royal Garden Party!" she fin-

ished triumphantly. "I'm so thrilled about the prospect of meeting royalty."

"Why? You've never been too impressed with me."

Elizabeth sighed. "Here we go again. *My great-grandmother was a Cherokee princess.* Sorry, Jake, it's just not the same, somehow." Jake Adair said very little about being Cherokee, but occasionally he liked to remind his colleagues of his noble origins.

"Okay." Jake shrugged. "I won't wear my ceremonial headdress to your wedding."

"I hope I have your word on that," said Elizabeth. "Tribal pageantry just won't fit into my plans for the ceremony."

"But kilts you've got?" he said, laughing. "I wouldn't miss this wedding for the world. Now I understand the part about the Queen. And I remember meeting the groom-to-be. Dr. Dawson from marine biology, right?"

Elizabeth nodded.

"But you're getting married *where?*"

"Chandler Grove, Georgia."

"You're not from Georgia."

"Used to be," said Elizabeth. "My parents moved away when I was in high school, so I don't really have any friends in the town where they live."

"Why not here at the university where your friends are?"

"No. I couldn't possibly manage all the arrange-

ments by myself. Besides, if I were here, I'd be distracted by work in the department."

"That seems unlikely," said Jake, nodding toward
the pile of books on the royal family. "But why not
get married in Scotland?"

"Would *you* know where to find a caterer in Scotland? No? Well, neither would I. Believe me, my aunt
Amanda is the only person in the world who could
stage a formal wedding on such short notice, and *she's*
in Chandler Grove. Besides, I'd trust Georgia's
weather over Scotland's any day."

"Okay. Never mind that's it a six-hour drive for all
of *us*. We'll carpool. Just don't expect us to wear morning coats."

"Kilts will do." Elizabeth grinned.

"About that ceremonial headdress . . ."

"Business suits will be fine, Jake."

"So that's settled. As I see it, you have just one
more problem." Jake looked grave. "Have you told
the Big Zee about all this?"

"No," said Elizabeth faintly. "I had forgotten all
about him."

"Lucky you," said Jake.

The Big Zee, as department chairman Ziffel was
known to his staff, was a man of little imagination and
less humor. He would not be amused—or even
civil—about Elizabeth's proposed defection from her
duties as an instructor for the summer term. "And

remember that you've got to face him for your orals this fall," Jake added ominously. "You'll be lucky if he doesn't pass *your* skull around the room for analysis."

Elizabeth looked close to tears. "It's only one morning course," she said piteously. "Eight A.M. Any of us could teach it."

"Yeah, but Mary Clare is gone for the summer, and I've agreed to play racquetball every morning with Laura Williams—oh, no. Don't look at me like that. I need this exercise, and besides, Laura Williams—" He sighed. "All right. I'll teach the damned course for you. But *you're* going to have to tell Ziffel."

Elizabeth nodded. "That's nothing," she said. "I'm going to have to tell Milo."

Jake patted her shoulder. "Oh, yes. The old boyfriend. Don't worry, kid. He'll get over it. How do *you* feel?"

"Very much like Cinderella," said Elizabeth. "I have a lot of messy jobs to do before I can go to the ball."

CHAPTER

4

IT HAD NOW BEEN several days since Cameron
Dawson had become a groom-to-be, and he was beginning to feel comfortable with the idea. Upon re-
flection, he decided that he rather liked the fact that
Elizabeth cared so passionately about things. Enthusiasm was something he generally lacked, having always been a bit of a plodder. He found it intoxicating

to be with someone whose emotions came in primary colors, rather than in his own muted shades of prudence, moderation, and practicality.

He could imagine Elizabeth rushing about to learn everything she could about the royal family (just as she had *done* the Brontës, harp seals, and Clan Chattan in previous binges). She would be enjoying herself hugely. And of course the wedding would be her own Broadway production. Cameron was relieved to be on the quiet side of the Atlantic while plans for *that* got under way.

He looked out at the steady drizzle of an Edinburgh summer afternoon. Where Elizabeth was, in Virginia, it would be blazing hot under a shimmering blue sky. He wondered if climate influenced human personalities, or if it only seemed so in this case.

Cameron had put on his gray lambswool sweater. (Elizabeth went into peals of laughter once when he'd called it a *jumper.* Apparently, in America a jumper was some sort of dress.) He hadn't wanted to put on the heat in the sitting room, for fear of complaints that he was being spoiled by living abroad. *Heat?* they would say. *In June?*

He was sitting at his mother's pigeonhole desk with her address book for Christmas cards, trying to decide whom to invite to the wedding. Not that he thought anyone would actually fly to the United States to see him star in a ten-minute ceremony, but he supposed that some folks would feel left out if he didn't notify them of the occasion.

The front door slammed. That would be Ian. While he was off from the university he was working part-time as a clerk and general dogsbody for an estate agent a few streets away. "It's pissing down out there!" he called from the hallway. "Have you brought the cat in?"

"What?" said Cameron, who was concentrating on postal codes. "No. I haven't seen him."

Ian appeared in the doorway in a shabby green mac, dripping pellets of rain on the carpet. "Well, he's getting quite old and Mother doesn't want him out when it's cold and wet."

The Dawson family cat was a dignified sealpoint Siamese nearly twenty years old. He had been given to Ian as a third birthday present by their American neighbors, the Carsons, whose own cat had unexpectedly presented them with a litter during their yearlong stay in Edinburgh. Dr. Carson, who was guest-lecturing in American history at the university at the time, had called the kitten Traveller Lee, after the horse of his favorite Confederate general, Robert E. Lee. For years kitty Traveller had slept in Ian's room in a doll bed donated by one of the Carson's daughters, but now the old Siamese was arthritic and frail, and he preferred to curl up near a radiator, if denied the warmth of Ian's lap.

"I haven't seen him," said Cameron. "Are you sure he isn't up in your room?"

"I'll check." Ian clumped up the stairs, yelling for the cat, and came down again seconds later. "Nope. He's out, and probably narky about it as well. I'll have a look in the garden."

Cameron went back to his list. That was the trouble with foreign brides, he thought. If she mailed the invitations to Scotland, the postage would cost a fortune, but it would spare him several hours of drudgery. As it was, she was sending him a package of printed invitations to do with as he wished, which would mean hours of folding and addressing, not to mention the chore of figuring out whom to ask in the first place. Adam McIver's name was next on the list. *Serve him right*, thought Cameron, copying out his address.

Another door slammed, the back one this time, and presently Ian appeared carrying a towel from which Traveller's little black face peered anxiously. "Found him," said Ian. "He was under the forsythia bush, and he was in an awful bate about being cast out into the storm. Turn on the heat, won't you, while I dry him off."

He knelt on the hearth and rubbed the tea-colored fur while Traveller licked a paw and cleaned his whiskers.

"He's a marvel for his age," said Cameron affectionately.

"Which is more than we can say for you," said Ian. "You'd left one of your magazines out in the garden."

"Sorry, I've got a lot on my mind."

Ian folded up the towel and left Traveller attending to his toilette on the hearth rug. "That's odd," he murmured, going to the window that faced onto the garden.

"What's odd?" asked Cameron, still scribbling.

"I knew something was the matter," announced Ian, peering through the rain-flecked window at the green expanse of lawn. "But I couldn't place what it was while I was out there. I was too busy getting wet. But I've realized it just now. Have you noticed that our garden gnome is missing?"

Cameron was still contemplating his list of prospective wedding guests. What about former roommates? Should you invite them? "I'm sorry. What did you say?" he murmured.

"The bloody *garden gnome!*" said Ian impatiently. "You know, the plaster one in the little red hat that used to stand over there next to the rowan tree. About three feet high and damned heavy, too. Well, he's gone missing."

Cameron went over to the window and looked out, but there was no sign of a plaster lawn ornament anywhere in the garden. "I hadn't noticed. Perhaps he's in the garage."

"No, I put my bike in there when I came home just now, and he isn't there."

"Well, perhaps he's been shifted to some other part of the lawn and you can't see him from here."

"I haven't moved him, and Mother certainly wouldn't, because he's too heavy for her to lift. Have you done something with him?"

"No, of course not," said Cameron. "I barely noticed the thing. It's vandals, I expect. Report it to the police or something, if you're that incensed about it."

"I certainly am," said Ian. "It's a violation of property. At the estate agents where I work they take that sort of thing very seriously. They're always cautioning me to look around the grounds when I show a house, to see if anything has been tampered with. Sometimes so-called pranks like that indicate that vandals have noticed the place. It's sort of a test, and if no action is taken over a small incident, they may come back and do much worse. We could be burgled."

"I suppose you're right," said Cameron. "I think you ought to phone the authorities."

Ian reddened. "I'd feel like an utter twit ringing up to report the theft of a garden gnome. They might think I actually liked the wretched statue."

"No, it's the principle of the thing. A poor gnome, but mine own," said Cameron with all the solemnity he could muster. "Besides, Mother likes it, doesn't she?"

Ian considered the matter. "She wouldn't get rid of it," he said at last. "It was a gift to her from Auntie Barbara. They used to go completely mad every spring planning the garden, remember? Always putting in cabbage roses, or some other improbable plant, and thinking up projects that required *us* to dig. The gnome was from their Tolkien period: *fairies at the bottom of the garden.*"

"True," said Cameron, smiling. "That makes the thing a family heirloom. I think you'd better notify the police."

"Why don't you call them? You're older."

"But you discovered the theft."

In the outer hall the telephone began to ring.

"Tell you what," said Cameron, moving toward the doorway. "Whoever the phone is for has to call the police when he's finished talking."

"That's hardly fair. You're only visiting, but I have dozens of friends who—oh, all right. It's a deal."

"Good. I thought it was your job to call anyhow." Cameron picked up the phone. "Dawson residence."

"Hello," said Elizabeth. "Did the invitations arrive yet?"

Cameron swore.

"Is anything the matter?" asked Elizabeth. "Why is someone laughing in the background?"

"Oh, never mind. No, the invitations have not arrived, but I'm working on my list."

"Good. I have finished sending out all the ones over here. All that's left is to plan the ceremony itself, but that will have to wait until I get to Chandler Grove. Meanwhile I've been reading royal biographies—you know, to get some ideas."

Cameron groaned.

"What did you say?"

"Oh, nothing. Reading royal biographies, are you?"

"Yes. They had such interesting lives. Did you know that Queen Mary—Princess May of Teck, she was then—was actually engaged to the older brother of George V, and when he died, she married George instead!"

"I'll have to mention that to Ian," said Cameron. *That will frighten him*, he finished silently.

"And, of course, I'm doing what I can to make preliminary plans for the wedding. At the moment I'm trying to decide what everybody is going to wear. Military dress uniforms would be wonderful, of course."

"I don't think they'd suit you, dear."

Elizabeth giggled. "You are in a temper, aren't you? Anyway, I don't suppose that you and Ian own kilts."

"Yes. I believe they're upstairs in a trunk in the box room. We had our pictures taken in them when we were nine and three respectively."

In the sitting room, Ian, who was eavesdropping,

had turned a strangled red in his efforts to keep quiet. *No kilts*, he mouthed soundlessly to his brother.

"I think we'll just wear suits, Elizabeth," said Cameron firmly. "Ian doesn't seem terribly taken with the idea of donning a kilt."

The brisk tone of Cameron's voice finally registered with his fiancée. "Is anything the matter, Cameron?" she asked. "You seem awfully strange."

Cameron sighed. "Oh, nothing major. I just have to ring up the police in a moment."

"The police!" cried Elizabeth. "What's wrong!"

"Nothing like *last* time you were in Edinburgh," Cameron assured her, remembering the evening that had ended with a murder in Tanner's Close. "Just a kidnapping this time. Someone has gone and stolen our garden gnome."

"Your what?"

"A plaster statue of a dwarf that used to stand in the garden in lieu of anything actually ornamental. Someone has taken it, apparently. Ugly thing. Our first impulse was to dash off a thank-you note to the thief, but Mother is actually fond of the thing, and Ian-the-Estate-Agent-Extraordinaire seems rather annoyed by the principle of the thing. Violation of property and all that. I suppose he's right. Next time it could be something valuable that is stolen. So I said I'd report it."

"Good luck," said Elizabeth. "I suppose things are

going well with you if that garden gnome is your biggest worry at the moment."

"Well, it makes for a change anyway," said Cameron.

◆ ◆ ◆

IN THE CHANDLER Grove Shrine to the U.S. Navy (also known as his study), Captain Grandfather was taking his afternoon nap, his swivel chair tilted back at a precarious angle and his feet propped up on the pine coffee table. Any lurching of the chair caused by the restless sleeper was translated by his dreams into the pitch of a ship at sea.

Soundlessly the study door opened, and the old man's grandson Charles crept in, moving in the exaggerated slow motion of one who is afraid of disturbing a sleeper. He was holding his breath as well. For a few seconds he looked about the room, exhaling slowly, and then breathing again, normally but quietly. His gaze slid past the ship models, the black-framed photographs, and the pile of unanswered letters, and finally lit upon the object of his quest: the current issue of *The Georgian Highlander*, an upscale local magazine, full of restaurant ads and notices of cultural events, neither of which interested Charles in the least. Nevertheless, it was vital that he get hold of the

magazine, which was at present lying on the coffee
table under Captain Grandfather's left foot.

After a few moments of deliberation, during which
he tried to think of an excuse for wanting the magazine
should he be caught filching it, Charles gently lifted
the old man's foot just enough to slide the *Highlander*
out. That accomplished, he replaced the foot on the
coffee table and crept out of the room.

He stopped by the kitchen for a glass of fruit juice
to fortify him as he worked, and then he hurried upstairs to his room with the purloined magazine.
Charles was inept at acting nonchalant and he was sure
he would look guiltier reading the innocuous *Highlander* than a bishop would with a copy of *Hustler*.

Once safely barricaded behind the door of his bedroom, Charles sat down at his desk and opened the
magazine. Flipping past the film reviews, the sym-
phony schedule, and the restaurant ads, he turned to
a part of the magazine that he had heretofore only
glanced at: the personals column. The editors called
this feature DSS, which apparently stood for Desperately Seeking Someone, and it was placed well toward the back of each issue. It had once been a source
of amusement to Charles that people could be so desperate for companionship that they would advertise
for a blind date, but now he felt the need to consult
the listings for reasons of his own. Of course, he would
have to check with the family attorney before doing

anything rash, but surely he could commit himself to the extent of composing a letter.

Charles skimmed the list of ads and discovered that his first task would be to decipher the code in which they were written. A closer examination proved that this was not difficult. It was just a local singles column, after all, not the Nobel Prize Winners' Sperm Bank. The initials SWF meant *single, white female.* He would begin with that category, and if he found nothing helpful there, he could go on to DWF, WWF, and whatever else the alphabet had to offer. He turned to the first entry.

SWF, the ad began, *Bible college grad, 32, seeks—* Charles stopped there. He didn't care *what* she sought; he wasn't about to contemplate a relationship with somebody who insisted that the world was created on a Tuesday in October in 2846 B.C.

What else was there?

WWF, 62, full-figured— Next!

. . . Professional, stable, enjoys movies, outdoor activities, quiet times . . . That sounded promising. Charles read the entry again. Oh. SW*M.* He might have known.

SWF, 22, out for a good time. Seeks laughs, travel, good dancer. Not ready to settle down—

Charles sighed in disgust. Where were all the eligible women in the world when he needed one? Here he was a veritable prize: he could cook; he could arrange flowers; he could show an intelligent interest in their careers. And did anyone care? No. All girls seemed to want these days were cheap, casual relationships with no responsibilities.

Charles read on. *DWF, likes movies . . .* Why did they all start by saying they liked movies? Surely no one was so pitiful as to need a companion just to sit in the dark and stare at a screen. Wasn't there anybody whose company would be preferable to a movie?

He stopped and took a gulp of fruit juice. It was, appropriately enough, passion punch. Maybe he was being too choosy with the personal ads. How much can one reveal about oneself in a one-inch box, after all? Besides, it wasn't as if he had much time to complete his plan. He stared up at the poster on the wall above his desk: a photograph of Albert Einstein against a background of the Horseshoe nebula. The caption, a quote from the great scientist, read: *God Does Not Play Dice with the Universe.* Charles wondered if that applied to biology as well as quantum physics. On an individual level, he doubted it. With a renewed sense of desperation, he returned to the DSS column.

This one looked promising. *Blonde SWF, 26, 5'7", 118 lbs. Good career in scientific field. Pretty, but no time to meet men. No married creeps. No serial killers. Someday my prince will come, but he'll have to find me. DSS-5-270690. The Georgia Highlander.*

That was more like it, thought Charles with a nod of satisfaction. He certainly seemed to fit most of her requirements—i.e., he hadn't been married and he had never murdered anyone. He wasn't so sure about the rest of her specifications, but nevertheless he allowed himself to fantasize about this perfect woman and found himself, as usual, picturing Sally Ride. Unfortunately, Dr. Ride (wherever she was these days) had better things to do than to be courted by a floundering physicist with not a single journal article to his credit. Perhaps this younger, obviously lonely young woman would recognize his potential and encourage him. Perhaps she would even be a physicist and could share his dreams!

Perhaps she would be Jane Goodall and think he was a perfect chimpanzee when she read his letter.

Charles tried not to give in to his natural pessimism. There was nothing to do but write a letter in response to her ad. He must try to sound intelligent, charming, sophisticated. (Is that what glamorous blondes were after these days?) Unfortunately, Charles had very little practice in two-thirds of those attributes. Intelligent he could be. He had been reading *Popular Electronics* since second grade, and his grades (except in literature) were effortlessly good. He didn't see why everybody made such a fuss about things like calculus; mathematics seemed perfectly straightforward to him. But perhaps his intellectual good qualities would not be endearing to this modern Athena. Charming and sophisticated he had never tried to be. That was Geoffrey's department. For a fleeting moment, Charles considered enlisting Geoffrey's help in composing the letter reply, but he dismissed the thought almost at once. If he told Geoffrey *why* he was doing it, it would spoil the whole plan, and if he pretended to be in search of a lady love, Geoffrey would laugh like a drain. The potential humiliation wasn't worth it.

He read the article again for clues as to the lady's preferences, but found nothing useful. He wished he had more to go on. It was difficult to make yourself attractive to someone you knew nothing about. Creative writing wasn't his forte anyhow.

With a sigh of resignation, Charles extracted a sheet of writing paper from the desk drawer and stared down at it, hoping for inspiration. None was forthcoming. The sheet lay there smugly, daring him to jot down an equation or two to break up the expanse of emptiness.

What should he call her? *Dear SWF* seemed accurate, but crass. *Dear Fellow Scientist* sounded like a fund-raising letter from the greenhouse effect people. He glanced at the ad. *Someday my prince will come. . . .* That was a line from a fairy tale wasn't it? Disney movie? Dredging up memories of long-forgotten kiddie matinees, Charles finally placed the reference. *Dear Snow White*, he wrote carefully. *I hope to become your prince.*

He nodded approvingly to himself. Not bad for an inarticulate physicist, he thought. Not even to himself did Charles ever say the word *nerd*.

◆　◆　◆

THAT EVENING IN Edinburgh Margaret Dawson was having tea with the ladies' circle from the church. (The primary item on the agenda was the forthcoming bazaar.)

Margaret's sons, left to fend for themselves, had managed to brew a pot of tea around five o'clock and were making do with leftover pastries from yesterday, rather than attempting any actual cooking themselves. They were counting on a substantial meal later that evening to compensate for this temporary deprivation. A roast on the top shelf of the refrigerator seemed to substantiate their hopes in this matter. (Unfortunately, neither of these college-educated louts had noticed the note tacked to the door of the refrigerator, which read: *Please put roast in oven on setting of gas mark 6 at 4:30. Love Mother.*)

Blissfully unaware of the coming famine, Ian Dawson had finished off a plate of shortbread and was sitting at the kitchen table watching the now-recovered Traveler tuck into his evening meal of whitebait when Cameron came in from the hall and poured himself a cup of tea, ignoring Ian completely. He carefully poured milk into the mug and stirred it, humming tunelessly. He started to put the milk jug into the refrigerator and then set it back down on the counter. "I keep forgetting that in this country, you don't have to refrigerate milk," he murmured. "When I first got to America, I tried leaving the milk out after breakfast. It didn't last a bloody day." He set his mug on the table, picked up the evening paper, and sat down to read it.

"Well?" said Ian impatiently. "What did they say about the gnome theft?"

"Who?" said Cameron, turning a page.

"The police, twit. Are they coming 'round?"

Cameron sighed and set aside the paper. "If you're so interested, Ian, you should have rung them up yourself."

Ian grinned. "A bet's a bet. Don't be such a bad sport. *Are* they coming to investigate?"

"No. They took the information over the telephone. After all, there really isn't anything for them to see. They just cautioned us to keep the house locked and to be especially careful for the next few days, in case the intruder comes back."

"I suppose that makes sense. I wonder who would take a garden gnome. Did they have any theories? Did they laugh?"

Cameron shook his head. "They have no sense of humor. And no theories, either. The officer I talked to was probably younger than you are. It was all one to him. You might check with a few of your rowdier friends, though, to see if this qualifies as a collegiate prank."

"I'll ask. But it doesn't seem likely."

"The whole thing seems unlikely."

"Well," said Ian, "this will be quite a blow to Mother. Losing a son *and* a garden gnome all in the same week."

CHAPTER

5

OF ALL THE ROYAL palaces used by the monarchs
of Scotland, only the palace of Holyroodhouse in
Edinburgh is still used for royal hospitality and cer-
emonies. The Queen devotes most of her time in
Scotland to her personal residence in the Highlands,
Balmoral Castle, where she stays on holiday for ten
weeks from early August until mid-October; but the

Queen's annual *official* visit to Scotland takes place
in early July, at which time she occupies the nine-
hundred-year-old palace of Holyroodhouse. It is a
turreted, sandstone building, made gloomy by
its deep-set windows and thick walls, and perhaps
echoing the sorrows of its principal resident, Mary,
Queen of Scots.

The original structure was an abbey, erected in the
twelfth century by King David of Scotland upon the
command of heaven. According to legend, King
David insisted upon going hunting on the day of the
Holy Rood (September 14), instead of spending the
day in prayer and contemplation of the Cross (or
Rood). During the hunt in the fields below Edinburgh
Castle, the king became separated from his huntsmen,
and he was thrown from his horse at the feet of an
angry stag, its head lowered to gore him. Suddenly a
mist enveloped the king, and when he put out his hand
to ward off the attacking animal, he found himself
grasping a cross between the antlers of the deer. The
animal ran away—and King David resolved to build
an Augustinian monastery, the Abbey of Holyrood,
on the site of the miracle. In later years, Robert the
Bruce held parliaments there.

In 1502, King James IV converted some of the
structures into a royal residence in honor of his marriage to Margaret Tudor, sister of England's King
Henry VIII. This union of the thistle and the rose was

celebrated at Holyrood, and the palace was further enlarged during the reign of their son James V. The abbey, destroyed in the "rough wooing" of the English in 1544, fell into ruins and was never rebuilt; only the foundations and the ruined nave of the church remain. The palace itself was rebuilt after the English invasion, and the daughter of James V—Mary, Queen of Scots— took up residence there in 1561. The nineteen-year-old Queen, already the widow of the King of France, married Lord Darnley in the Chapel Royal, and it was in Holyrood that the Queen's secretary, David Rizzio, was murdered by Darnley and his men.

After Mary's son, James VI, left Scotland to inherit the throne of Elizabeth I of England, the castle was abandoned by royalty for nearly two centuries. Bonnie Prince Charlie held court there during his ill-fated attempt to seize the throne, but it was not until the nineteenth century that another monarch took any interest in the palace. Queen Victoria, who loved all things Scottish, restored Holyroodhouse, and made it her custom to stay there once yearly, a tradition that has been continued by her descendants to this day.

During her week in residence at the palace of Holyroodhouse, the Queen is welcomed to the city by being presented with the keys of the city of Edinburgh in the Ceremony of the Keys, held in the west front courtyard. It is during this week that the Queen presides over the Ceremony of the Thistle—the Scottish equivalent of the Order of the Garter—in nearby St. Giles Cathedral.

She also hosts a tea party on the grounds of the palace of Holyroodhouse. With eight thousand guests, the event is about as intimate as a rock concert, but it is a singular honor to be invited—and the manicured lawns of the palace are lovely, as are the views of Arthur's Seat and Salisbury Crag, majestic in the distance.

Cameron Dawson's memories of the palace of Holyroodhouse are unfortunately centered on sheep droppings.

"Sheep droppings?" said Elizabeth, staring at the telephone as if it had misquoted the caller. Several days had passed since their last conversation, and she was phoning to report on the wedding progress, and to augment her newly acquired knowledge of things royal.

"Yes," said Cameron, after the usual transatlantic pause. "You know, those little brown pellets that tell you where sheep have been . . ."

"In the *palace?*"

"No, of course not in the palace, twit. But just outside the gates of the palace and off to the right there is a rugby field belonging to the Royal High School. At least they use it for rugby. Apparently sheep also have the run of the field. Anyhow, when I was at Fettes—"

"You played rugby?" asked Elizabeth, momentarily distracted from contemplation of the palace.

"Yes, in the seventeenth fifteen."

"What does that mean?"

"It means I was an abysmal rugby player. The first fifteen is what you'd call the varsity, I suppose. They play in the school stadium and represent the school. And then you had a second team of fifteen players, and a third fifteen and so on."

"And you were on team number *seventeen?*"

"Yes."

"I suppose that's why you played against sheep."

"The better teams were made up of boys at higher grade levels than mine," said Cameron reproachfully. "And I was rather thin in those days."

"Get back to the sheep."

"We played a Saturday-morning game against the Royal High School team on that field near the palace. I played fullback, where you stayed back and hoped the other team didn't try to score. *Nobody* wanted to be tackled during that game because, as I said, the sheep used that field a lot more than the rugby team had. Of course, the other team's colors were black and white, so there was a chance it mightn't have shown up . . ."

"I trust the sheep won't be grazing on the site of the garden party."

"I doubt it, but you might want to wear brown shoes just in case."

Elizabeth decided to ignore him. "Is it all set, then, about my going?"

"I think so. I hunted up Adam McIver, and he said he'd see what he could do."

"Will we be able to go inside the palace?"

"Well, you can't do as the sheep do, if that's what you mean. But you won't be able to wander about looking at tapestries, either. No tours while the royal family is in residence. It's just an ordinary castle— paneled walls, paintings right and left, you know— the usual decor. Now, perhaps, at transatlantic phone prices, we ought to talk about the wedding."

"All is well. The invitations are being printed; the department head has been placated; and the engagement announcement has gone out to the newspapers. I leave for Chandler Grove tomorrow. How are things in Scotland?"

"As far as wedding plans? No problem. Plane reservations are made and we've made all the phone calls to the relatives."

"Solved your kidnapping yet?" asked Elizabeth.

"What, the gnome? No, but it's the damnedest thing!"

"What?"

"We got a postcard from him today."

"You did? From the thief?"

"No," said Cameron dryly. "From the gnome."

"I didn't know it knew its address. What does the postcard say?"

There was a pause and then Cameron, obviously reading from the card in question, intoned: "*Decided to go on holiday. Having wonderful time. Wish you were here.—(Signed) Your Garden Gnome.* It's addressed to *The Dawsons.*"

"Where is he?"

"The postcard is from Ibiza, and the stamps are Spanish. Postmarked there three days ago."

Elizabeth burst out laughing. "Are you going after him?"

"No. I think that all our traveling will be in another direction. To the state of Georgia, to be exact. I told someone at church where I was getting married and he said, '*In the Soviet Union?*'"

"Yes, we tend to forget that they have a Georgia, too."

"The accents are similar," said Cameron.

Elizabeth ignored this gibe. "It will be wonderful to see your mother and Ian again."

"Mother's looking forward to her first visit to the States. She's mad to do some sightseeing. Wants to know where she's staying."

Elizabeth smiled to herself. "You all are going to use my aunt Louisa's place. It's across the road from the Chandlers'."

"Your auntie's place. I see. And what's it like?"

"Oh, it's just an ordinary castle—paneled walls, paintings right and left. You know—the usual."

◆   ◆   ◆

IN THE FROZEN-FOODS aisle of the Chandler Grove Piggly Wiggly, Tommy Simmons was reading the nutritional information on the back of the micro-waveable dinners. He supposed he ought to get into the habit of preparing real food, but there didn't seem to be any point in cooking for one. Besides, people often took pity on his bachelor status and invited him out to dinner. Most of these dinners required him to give free legal advice on some minor matter, such as whether the owners of amorous tomcats could be made to pay child support for the resulting kittens (*no*), but Tommy didn't mind. It made a nice change from land transfers and will drafting.

Perhaps he ought to try the *diet* frozen dinners, he thought, blanching at one five-hundred-calorie pasta entree. Just lately people had been exhibiting a regrettable tendency to overestimate his age. A sophomore from the local high school had tried to interview him on details of the Korean War. As if he'd admit to being on the *planet* during the Korean War! He blamed it on the Simmons family physique, which tended toward short stature and nonexistent

♦

waistlines. His hairline wasn't much help, either; he was going bald on top, which only increased his resemblance to Friar Tuck. If the low-calorie cuisine didn't improve matters, Tommy was afraid that he might have to invest in a videocassette and seek help from another Simmons: Richard, to whom he was not related.

He was just heading toward the produce section to purchase massive quantities of lettuce when a gaunt individual with an armload of herbal-tea packages backed into his cart. Not wishing to contemplate hit-and-run, the lawyer eased his shopping cart to the side of the aisle and rushed forward to see to the plaintiff.

"Are you all right?" he asked, for the fellow did look alarmingly pale. "I'm afraid you didn't see me coming."

"Oh, I'm fine. The velocity of that thing wasn't—" Glowing dark eyes looked down into Tommy Simmons's round face. "Hey, aren't you the family lawyer? Makes you want to believe in synchronicity, doesn't it? I was just thinking about you."

Tommy would have willingly returned the compliment, but he had no idea whom he was addressing. "Well, it's nice to see you," he ventured. The dark-haired young man was dressed in jeans and a gray sweatshirt. He could be anybody.

"Thank you. I wasn't sure you'd remember me. I

guess lawyers have to have a good memory, but I'm flattered all the same."

Inwardly, Tommy Simmons groaned. When someone said that, it was impossible to admit that you had absolutely no idea who they were. The only conceivable course of action was to keep the conversation going as neutrally as possible, and to hope that further clues would be forthcoming. At times like this, Tommy was haunted by the tale of an Atlanta colleague who had experienced just such a memory lapse once while talking to an elderly woman at a reception. After a few pleasantries, the woman had mentioned her son, and grasping at this clue to her identity, the fellow had exclaimed, "Oh, yes, your *son*. What's he doing these days?" To which Lillian Carter had replied, "Oh, he's still president of the United States."

"Well, how have you been?" asked Tommy, casting about for safe topics of inquiry.

"All right, I guess. There's not much to do around here, though. And the public library is most deficient in the sciences."

Tommy endeavored to look sympathetic. Then, noticing the boxes of herbal tea, he said, "Well, there's nothing I can do about the library, but I can recommend another place for you to grocery-shop. Did you know that a health-food place has opened in the old gristmill?"

◆

The stranger looked interested. "No kidding! Macrobiotic stuff?"

"Er . . . probably," said Tommy, who wouldn't have shopped there at gunpoint. "Kelp and trail mix and that sort of thing. It's called Earthlings. You should check them out."

"Thanks, I will." Tommy had intended for that to be the end of the encounter, but the young man steadied the tea boxes, making no attempt to move on. "Listen, there's something I need to ask you." He cast furtive glances up and down the aisle of the supermarket. "Just a quick question, really. Do you think you could answer it off the top of your head—without having to consult files in your office, I mean?"

"I don't know," said Tommy, eyeing his frozen food with some concern. "I could try."

"It's about my great-aunt Augusta's will. You looked into the matter a couple of years ago when my sister Eileen—just before she—"

Tommy managed to suppress a smile of triumph. He had it! Charles Chandler! A bit more scruffy and gaunt than he remembered, but the family resemblance had struck him at last. "Yes, Charles," he said smoothly. "I do recall that instance. What would you like to know about the will?"

"I wondered about the wording. You know, the circumstances required to inherit."

"It was strange, wasn't it?" said Tommy, nodding.

"A classic case of the vindictive will. Some people love to take parting shots. Apparently your great-aunt had married against her family's wishes and her fortune derived from that action."

Charles blinked. "I guess you could say that. I heard that her husband died and she invested his money in California real estate. It's all in trust now, though."

"Yes. Apparently she wanted to remind the family that affairs had turned out for the best, despite their opinions to the contrary. Never mind that most of those who opposed her marriage had predeceased her."

"Well, her brother—that's my grandfather—is still around. But he hasn't changed his mind, either."

"Anyway, according to the terms of her will, she, being childless, left the money to whichever of her great-nieces or nephews should marry first."

"*Marry* first," said Charles. "Not just get engaged?"

"Correct. Remember, your sister was formally engaged before her unfortunate passing." Tommy preferred not to utter the word *death*—just as he managed to avoid most of the other one-syllable expressions of Anglo-Saxon derivation. It was a natural inclination, fortified by his training in the law. "Remember that her fiancé did not receive the bequest."

Charles nodded. "True. Okay, so you have to be legally married. No stipulations other than that?"

"I'd have to double-check, but I think the answer is no."

"How much is the estate worth now?"

"Now *that* I would have to look up," said Tommy, edging toward his grocery cart. "But considering what has happened to California real estate in recent years, I'd say well over a million. Yes, that's safe to say. I think you could sell a doghouse in Los Angeles for that."

Charles grabbed the attorney's hand and shook it enthusiastically. "Thanks!" he cried. "You've been a great help!"

"No, not at all. You're entitled to know." Tommy could hear the self-justification in his own voice, as if he were denying responsibility for the outcome of this discussion.

Tommy Simmons wheeled his cart toward the checkout counters with the inexorable feeling that while he may have been helpful to Charles Chandler, he had also just been a great nuisance to somebody else. He wondered who would suffer from Charles's newfound discovery.

◆   ◆   ◆

ALTHOUGH THE wedding of Elizabeth MacPherson was still more than ten days away, the atmosphere on the Chandler premises had begun to take on that

charged quality indicative of approaching thunder-
storms. Both Amanda and Mildred, the housekeeper,
had taken to following the other occupants about with
hand-held vacuum cleaners; the carpeting was clammy
from frenzied applications of rug shampoo; and the
smell of Murphy's Oil Soap lingered in the air.

Moreover, despite all attempts to convey to
Amanda their sincere and complete indifference to
the impending occasion, the male Chandlers were
endlessly regaled with the minutiae of the plans con-
cerning the decorations, the reception, and the cos-
tumes of the participants, themselves included.

In desperation Dr. Robert Chandler had invented
the necessity to rewrite chapter seven of his book on
the whim of his editor, who was conveniently away
on vacation in Nassau, unaware that he had been cast
as the villain of the charade. The fugitive author had
taken refuge in his study, ostensibly to complete this
vital task, with strict orders that he was not to be disturbed, and his wife supposed him to be toiling away
before the silent word processor in thrall to a deadline.
He was careful to keep the television volume turned
low and to hide his cache of Louis L'Amour novels
behind the filing cabinet in case of unannounced visits
from the wedding terrorists.

The doctor's companion in exile was Valerian, an
imposing Maine Coon Cat, whose shaggy and shed-
ding dark coat had thrown him into disfavor with the

current regime. After having been driven from the sofa, the armchair, and even the carpeted staircase by cleaning fanatics, the feline emperor had demanded asylum by scratching on the door of the doctor's study and meowing piteous complaints about his ill-treatment. All eighteen pounds of him were now comatose and sprawled across the book galleys as he recuperated from the fatigue of an interrupted nap. His fellow refugee napped in the chesterfield chair by the window.

When someone tapped softly at the door of the study, Dr. Chandler awoke with a start—and with just enough presence of mind to thrust his paperback between the seat cushion and the arm of the chair. Valerian did not twitch so much as an eyelid.

"Come in!" called Dr. Chandler, scrambling to get to his desk. Unfortunately, his manuscript was buried under an avalanche of cat, so he endeavored to look busy with a yellow legal pad.

"Robert, I thought you might like some coffee," said his wife, appearing in the doorway with two cups and a plate of cookies on a newly polished silver tray. The tray and the fact that the cups were from a set of antique Bavarian china, usually kept in the bow-fronted display cabinet, were other signs of the rampant formality occasioned by the wedding.

"I see you plan to join me, dear," said Dr. Chandler, eyeing the second coffee cup. "How thoughtful."

The invasion having been accomplished with the utmost civility, Amanda set the tray on the glass-topped table and settled into the chesterfield chair with the air of one who is about to preside at a meeting. "How is your chapter coming?" she asked, handing him the plate of cookies.

"Oh, tolerably," he replied, glancing nervously at the cat. "It's painstaking work, you know."

"No. I cannot *think* why anyone would want to write a book. It pays very little and people only seem to read them in order to express unkind opinions about them." She shrugged. "Really, why bother? But you go right ahead with your little hobby. I just wanted to tell you how things were progressing with the wedding."

"Elizabeth isn't even here yet," he grumbled, thinking it only fair that the blushing bride should share in the general inconvenience.

"No, but that hardly matters, does it? Brides are a nuisance, anyway. They always come up with the most unsuitable ideas and often one has to be quite firm with them."

"Why shouldn't she have some say-so, Amanda? It's her wedding!"

Amanda laughed. "Really, Robert, you might as well ask the cow how it wants the roast cooked. Elizabeth will be wise to leave everything to me, as I have a great deal of experience in social matters. She did phone to ask about locating one of her old school friends from high school. Wants her for a bridesmaid."

"And were you able to assist her?"

"Oh, yes. She certainly isn't hard to find." Amanda paused for effect. "It's Jenny Ramsay."

Dr. Chandler thought hard. "That name sounds familiar. Have we met her?"

"Every day for four years, Robert. She's the weather girl on Channel Four."

"Oh! *Jenny*. The perky little blonde who does the parades and things."

"Exactly. Elizabeth hasn't seen her since high school, but apparently they'd made some sort of teenage promise to be bridesmaids at each other's wedding. I told you brides were dangerous."

"She'll look quite nice as a bridesmaid."

"Certainly she will." Amanda looked as if she wanted to add something, but apparently she thought better of it. "Oh, well!" she said with a little laugh. "Where was I? Oh, yes. I have made an appointment with Country Garden in Chandler Grove so that we can talk about the flowers—Elizabeth will be able to contribute to that discussion. And I have spoken to Mr. Compton at the community college about handling the photography. Now the caterers pose a bit of a problem. Lucy Bedford is on vacation this month and I had counted on using her. However, Charles recommended a new group in town. He has spoken

to them and they are coming out tomorrow, so perhaps it will be all right." Pushing her reading glasses
back on the top of her head, she took an appraising
look at her husband. "I'll need to take a look at you
in your black suit, dear. I did think that morning coats
might be nice, but we can't be sure of what the groom
is planning to wear. Possibly a kilt."

"He's on his own, then."

"He will have to be telephoned. I will delegate that
to Elizabeth. Now, is there anything else I've forgotten?"

"Are you *sure* this is all right with Doug and Margaret? She's their only daughter, you know."

Amanda looked thoughtful. "I imagine it's a great
relief, really. You know that Margaret's idea of formal
entertaining is two tables of bridge. Besides, I think
they may see it as a kindness."

"How's that?"

"Because we lost our little girl just before her wedding." To her husband's surprise, the brisk efficiency
dissolved into the faltering voice of one trying very
hard to overcome great obstacles.

Dr. Chandler kissed his wife's cheek. "If there's
anything I can do, Amanda, just let me know."

She patted his hand. "Thank you, Robert. I am man-
aging well enough right now. You go back to your
cowboy book." With that she picked up the tray and
was gone.

CHAPTER

6

ELIZABETH LOOKED at the collection of mismatched and battered luggage heaped on the pavement beside her car. Each suitcase and totebag bore an identifying label (*Cosmetics; Shoes; Stationery*) so that she could find the items she had flung inside in the little time she'd had to pack.

"If I were organized, I would be taking only half

this much," she mused. As it was, she had thrown *everything* into the baggage, just to make sure that she wasn't missing anything that would later turn out to be vital. She would have a difficult time fitting the untidy mound into her little car.

Elizabeth's one point of satisfaction in seeing the mismatched heap was its striking resemblance to a pile of luggage pictured in one of her ubiquitous books on the royal family (they were now stashed in a black canvas suitcase labeled *Books on Royal Family*). Someone had photographed the Queen's baggage at dockside, waiting to be loaded onto the royal yacht *Britannia*; there was a jumble of leather suitcases, cardboard boxes, green canvas bags, British Airways totebags, and black trunks, all bearing the yellow tag indicating that the items belong to the Her Majesty.

When she discovered the picture, Elizabeth had been surprised at how plebeian the royal luggage looked. Surely the Queen—by all accounts the richest woman in the world—ought to be able to afford better travel receptacles than that! She should have a set of handmade leather luggage. Twenty matching pieces— forty! It made you wonder about expressions like *fit for a queen*! At least Her Majesty never had to carry any of the bags herself. That is where she and I differ, thought Elizabeth, hoisting a quilted garment bag into the back seat.

It was going to be a long drive. In order to reach

Chandler Grove, located in the northernmost tip of
Georgia, a traveler from southwest Virginia could
either take Interstate 77 through the North Carolina
piedmont to Charlotte—three hours of mindless driving—or one could follow the Blue Ridge Parkway, a
rambling scenic route through the heart of the mountains, which took longer than the Lewis and Clark expedition. Elizabeth decided to take the dull but direct
route. There would be enough scenic country roads
after Charlotte, where anyone bound for Chandler
Grove had to veer to the right and scoot across the
South Carolina hills to pick up Highway 441 in Georgia. There, a succession of increasingly smaller country lanes led at last to Long Meadow Farm. The whole
trip took about six hours, during which time Elizabeth
planned to reflect further on her organization schemes
for the wedding.

I expect I'm being very silly, thought Elizabeth. *Probably some sort of genetic madness left over from the days
when it* mattered *whether you got married or not. But
it's* my *wedding, so whose business is it how manic I get?*

She had spent the past few days devouring volumes
on wedding etiquette, wedding folk customs, and
royal weddings, soaking up the details as if she were
going to be tested on the material. Now she was almost as much of an authority on the subject as Aunt
Amanda. "And probably equally tiresome," she said
aloud. Elizabeth had no illusions about the glamour

of romance; for nonroyal brides the fascination with matrimonial trivia did *not* extend beyond the bride's most immediate circle. (This did not include the groom.) But she thought that perhaps women made a great ceremonial event out of a wedding in hopes that they would have to do it only once in their lives.

The volumes on royal weddings fascinated Elizabeth. She decided that she would not borrow any ideas from the weddings of Princess Margaret or Princess Anne, because their marriages had not worked out. "Of course I'm being superstitious about it!" she told Jake Adair. "If you're not superstitious, why get married at all?" To which Jake suggested that she go down the hall to cultural anthropology and give herself up as a research specimen.

Elizabeth had begun her wedding research by reading a good deal about the wedding of Prince Charles and Lady Diana Spencer. She was delighted to learn that her wedding date, July first, was also the birthday of Princess Diana, but she soon found that reading about the wedding was depressing in more ways than one. First of all, nobody's wedding could bear comparison to that of the Prince of Wales, and in contrast it made even the most ambitious of efforts seem shoddy. What was Aunt Amanda's oak-paneled drawing room compared to the splendor of St. Paul's? And who cared whether your invitations were engraved or not, if *theirs* had been issued by the lord chamberlain on behalf of the Queen?

Once Elizabeth had got so caught up in her nuptial fantasies that she remarked aloud to Jake, "Would I love to get married in St. Paul's Cathedral!"

Jake looked up from his Tony Hillerman novel and said, "Why? You don't know anybody in Minnesota, do you?"

But there were drawbacks to the royal wedding that Elizabeth would not have to contend with. She comforted herself with those thoughts. No need of security guards. No government interference, forcing you to slight friends and distant relations in favor of foreign dignitaries. And nobody making the decisions for you about the reception food, the honeymoon, and all the other delightful details of planning the event. *Face it*, she told herself, *Diana had very little say-so in that wedding.*

Which brought her to the other depressing fact she had gleaned from her reading: by American standards the Princess of Wales was not even a high-school graduate. "*That* puts my Ph.D. in perspective," Elizabeth had remarked. She would gladly give Diana any number of IQ points if she could also transfer to the princess a pound of weight per point.

Why couldn't I be dumb and thin? she asked herself. Clearly, Princess Diana did not bear thinking about.

Thank God for Fergie.

The other royal wedding, that of Prince Andrew and Sarah Ferguson, had been much more to Elizabeth's liking. Elizabeth couldn't even daydream herself into the role of a svelte blonde ice princess marrying the heir apparent, but the plump and clever Duchess of York was a bride that she could identify with. She read the hastily published biographies of the newlyweds with considerable interest.

Sarah Ferguson was a full twenty-six when she married Prince Andrew. She had held a full-time job; she was definitely not a size five; and she'd had two past affairs that nobody troubled to deny. This was a far cry from the virginal teenage Princess of Wales; this was bordering on reality as Elizabeth knew it.

Elizabeth studied the details of the Yorks' wedding for inspiration. She liked the Duchess's wedding gown; its low-cut circular bodice was very flattering; just the thing for the full-figured bride. Elizabeth hoped she could find one of a similar design.

From a description of Sarah's bridal bouquet, Elizabeth learned that a sprig of myrtle was traditionally included for brides. (*Whatever for?*) Consult the folklore book. *Myrtle, the symbol of Venus, goddess of love.* Can you get sprigs of myrtle in June in Georgia? Elizabeth wondered. That should be an exciting task for the florist. What else should she use in her bouquet? Thistles, of course, for Scotland, and maybe dogwood, the state flower of Virginia. Subject, of course, to whatever the florists could manage on such short notice. *It's a good thing I didn't have more time*, Elizabeth admitted to herself; *I could have been a florist's nightmare.*

The one custom about a royal wedding that Elizabeth did not admire and envy was the use of small children as the members of the wedding party. "There is no way," she said, frowning at the charming photos of princes in sailor suits and winsome four-year-olds in Victorian frocks. "They'd probably start pelting each other with hymnbooks."

Not that the American custom of bridesmaids was much better. The bride was expected to choose her sister, her fiancé's sister, and a few close friends or cousins as attendants, preferably the most presentable looking of her acquaintances, so as not to blight the wedding pictures. Ruefully, Elizabeth remembered her own summons to serve as bridesmaid for Cousin Eileen, whom she barely knew. She had hated the malarial yellow dress chosen for her. *I'm as bad off as Eileen was*, she thought. *I don't have anybody to ask. How thoughtless of Cameron and me not to have sisters. We're all right on brothers: Ian and Bill, for best man and usher, and presumably Charles and Geoffrey can usher. But that presupposes having four woman attendants. Not possible.*

It was at this moment of desperation that Elizabeth remembered a childhood vow made with her then-best friend Jenny Ramsay, when during an orgy of sentiment watching *Pride and Prejudice* they had promised to be bridesmaids in each other's wedding. Elizabeth's family had moved to Virginia when she was in the tenth grade, so she and Jenny had not expereinced the caste system of high school together. Gradually they lost touch. She hadn't heard from Jenny in years. Elizabeth seemed to recall that she had gone to college at Agnes Scott—or was it Meredith? She remembered Jenny as a perky, fun-loving blonde whose idols in life were Donny Osmond and, in her *I Dream of Jeannie* days, Barbara Eden. Assuming that Jenny had not fulfilled her youthful dream of residing in a bottle in the home of an astronaut, she was probably still somewhere in the vicinity of Chandler Grove. (Burger King, thought Elizabeth uncharitably, remembering Jenny's grade-point average in junior high.)

When Elizabeth telephoned Aunt Amanda to ask about the whereabouts of Jenny Ramsay, she was surprised that her aunt recognized the name at once. She was even more surprised to learn that Jenny, far from sporting a paper hat and serving fast food, was part of the news team on the local television station. Elizabeth had written her a long chatty letter, summarizing a few years of achievements and adventures, and ended by telling her about the Queen's garden party and asking Jenny to be her maid of honor. The reply

arrived a few days later, on a cat notecard: *Love to!*
Call me when you get back to C. Grove!

So that was settled. Jenny for maid of honor and
Mary Clare from the anthropology department as a
bridesmaid. ("Be sure you take notes during the ceremony!" Jake had urged her.)

Elizabeth, busy with her plans, sped past the mountain vistas of I-77 and down into the pine forests of
middle Carolina with hardly a glance at the scenery.

◆   ◆   ◆

GEOFFREY DREW ASIDE the curtain and gazed out
at the winding gravel driveway. "I thought she'd be
here by now, didn't you?" he remarked to his brother
Charles. "Of course, the trip probably takes longer
with mice and pumpkin."

"Pumpkin?" said Charles, whose inattention was ev-
ident. "What are you talking about?"

"It was a literary reference. Remember Cinderella?
I was alluding to Cousin Elizabeth's fondness for
building castles in the air and then moving into them."

Charles did not bother to reply, as this might be
interpreted by Geoffrey as an inducement to stay.
Charles had retreated to the musty depths of the
Chandler library to commune with his thoughts, and
he had enjoyed a quiet hour of brandy and contemplation in the leather chair next to the fireplace. The

interruption by Geoffrey, who insisted upon pulling back the velvet curtains and peering out the window while making inane remarks, was most unwelcome. Charles had just completed some soul-searching and found to his chagrin that he had remarkably little area to cover. The depression resulting from this discovery had made the prospect of a visit with his adder-tongued brother even more painful than usual.

Geoffrey, blissfully unaware of the dread he inflicted, prattled on about the family's current obsession. "I should be learning my lines for the play, of course, but I doubt that I shall get much chance with all the distractions to come. Still, I expect that I shall find Elizabeth's royalty fantasies highly entertaining. Although, Lord knows, Southern brides are prone to it with less provocation than she has. Did you ever notice that?"

"What?" murmured Charles. He was holding his brandy snifter in both hands, as if he expected the spirits therein to offer the sort of career advice Macbeth had received.

"About Southern brides' royalty fantasies," said Geoffrey, warming to his topic. "A couple of weeks before the wedding, they all come down with a strange personality disorder. It's characterized by delusions of grandeur, obsession with ritual, and a tendency toward ruthless tyranny."

"I hadn't noticed."

"I expect you will, Charles. I predict that within hours of her arrival, Elizabeth will turn this place into the court of Catherine the Great. The brides can't help it, I suppose. Southern women are raised on rosy images of Scarlett O'Hara and all the beautiful belles of Southern mythology. You know, the fiery little minx who breaks men's hearts." He shuddered. "We tend to encourage that image of femininity, wouldn't you say?"

Charles shrugged. "I don't pretend to be an expert on femininity."

Geoffrey reddened. "Nor do I, but we in the theatre make it a point to study all of humankind. You should hear my analysis of *you*. But as I was saying, here are all these Southern girls, fancying that the best thing to be is a belle—only they are never given the opportunity. In today's world, there's college, dressing for success in your sensible job, and a social scene based on the *pretense* of equality, at least. Which is, of course, exactly what they desire—or ought to desire—but they have this peculiar idea drilled into their head by elderly female relatives that to be *feminine* is to be a silly, pouting coquette."

"Ugh," said Charles, whose idea of foreplay was the Mensa exam.

"I quite agree," purred Geoffrey. "And I do think that modern Southern women ignore this conditioning admirably well. The only time they really succumb to the belle fantasy is when they are about to become brides. That's when tradition takes over—"

"*Something old, something new . . .*" murmured Charles, sipping his drink.

"Something Scarlett," said Geoffrey. "The wedding belle. A formal wedding is every woman's chance to star in *Gone With the Wind*. For a few short weeks she is the bride, able to throw scenes, to make people wait on her, and to be the absolute center of attention. This is how she thinks she ought to behave. It has very little to do with the institution of matrimony, as far as I can tell. It's an ancient and terrible ritual. We're in for it, I tell you."

"So if Cousin Elizabeth starts throwing tantrums, we tell her to put a sock in it."

Geoffrey shook his head. "It's not going to be that easy."

Clearly intending that to be his exit line, Geoffrey strolled toward the door, but their conversation had reminded Charles of something. He motioned for his brother to stay. "Listen, before you go, there's something I wanted to ask you," he began awkwardly.

"Yes, Charles, what is it? Do say that you are asking me to recommend a good hairdresser, because I have been so hoping—"

Charles scowled and swept a dark forelock away from his eyes. "I don't need a haircut!"

◆

Geoffrey closed his eyes dramatically. "Perhaps a defoliant . . ."

"What I wanted to ask you was—" He was blushing furiously. "Oh, this is ridiculous. Never mind!"

"Now you *have* gained my attention," Geoffrey announced. "Out with it, Charles. What advice can I offer? A tailor's reference? Singing lessons, perhaps? Have you been mispronouncing wines?"

"No." Charles was sullen, as people usually were after more than ten minutes of Geoffrey Chandler. "I'd like to know how you meet girls around here."

His brother favored him with an acid smile. "In your case, Charles, I should recommend setting snares." This was Geoffrey's second attempt at an exit, but this time his curiosity got the better of him. "Just what *is* going on?" he demanded. "And why come to me? Surely you know that Mother would be delighted to throw you to the social wolves if you so much as indicated your willingness to go."

Charles paled. "No. I don't want to attend dances or anything like that. I'd just like to meet someone nice. It's time I thought about settling down with someone who's my type. You know, involved in the sciences."

"What a pity for you that Typhoid Mary is no longer with us." Geoffrey deemed that exit line too good to pass up, and so he left.

◆ ◆ ◆

JENNY RAMSAY WAS touched and pleased to hear from her old friend Elizabeth after so many years, but she did not share her friend's elation about a marriage day that coincided with the birthday of Princess Diana. In a way, Jenny had been Princess Diana for several years now and quite often she found it a royal pain.

This was one of those times.

As usual, she was impeccably dressed: pink linen suit, ruffled blouse with a satin ribbon at the neck, and her trademark double strand of cultured pearls. Her hair was a smooth, blonde bob, perfectly disciplined to stay in place, just short of her tiny gold earrings, and her heart-shaped face was carefully made up to look not made up at all. She wore her usual expression of sincere and urgent *interest*, suggesting that the present discussion of gardening strategies and shrubbery upkeep was the high point of her week.

In fact she was bored shitless. (*Not* an expression that anyone had ever heard Jenny Ramsay use, but she *thought* it a lot.) In her capacity as honorary chairperson and goodwill ambassador to the rest of Georgia, she was attending a board meeting of the local County Beautification Committee, and her fellow committee members had been holding forth for a good hour and a half, which is a long time to have to smile and look fascinated by utter drivel. Jenny was trying to think of a plausible yet foolproof way of escape.

Jenny Ramsay had graduated from college with a sorority pin, a C average, and a degree in communications, which she hoped to parlay into a career in show business. In the spring of her senior year, she had entered the local pageant of the Miss Georgia contest, in hopes of gaining some media attention, useful to job seekers who are short on marketable skills. Thanks to several years of aerobics classes with her sorority sisters, she looked all right for the swimsuit competition (though it felt rather strange to be parading around a crowded auditorium with hardly anything on). "Take out your contact lenses," a pageant official advised her. "It's a lot easier if the audience is just one big blur."

The evening-gown event was delightful. She had worn a turquoise ball gown that needed only a wand to make her look like a fairy princess, and she was sure that the judges gave her higher marks than anybody in that category.

Jenny's real problem with the pageant was the talent portion of the program. Jenny couldn't sing—and her notions of dancing involved a drunken DKE for a partner and a very loud dose of beach music. It was then that she discovered she had entered the pageant fifteen years too late. The true contenders had been competing since the age of four, when ambitious and farsighted mothers enrolled them in piano, ballet, and modern-dance classes. On the advice of one of her communications professors, Jenny ended up doing Emily in the last act of *Our Town*, but she lost the crown to a cellist from Milton's Forge, whose ambitions were to become a speech therapist and end world hunger.

The pageant had not been a total loss, however. One of the judges had been an executive from the local television station, and he had seen a perky quality in Jenny Ramsay that he thought would add just the right spark to the Channel Four news team. They already had the anchor duo—Bill (an overgrown Boy Scout) and Victoria (dark-haired and serious)—and sports announcer Badger Darnell, whose knee injury had sidelined him from a pro baseball career. Jenny was young and inexperienced, but the station thought that with a little coaching, Jenny Ramsay could corner the ratings for north Georgia.

She was hired to announce the weather on the six o'clock news, but although the public saw this as her principal function, it was, in fact, a small part of her duties, mostly involving reading prepared forecasts supplied to the station by actual meteorologists. Jenny's part in the process was to wear cute outfits, read the teleprompter with accuracy and convincing sincerity while pointing to the correct spot on the map (you *had* to know which one was Alabama and which one was Mississippi), and to function as the so-called little sister of the news team. Jenny was the one who cooed over feature stories about animals and who talked about snowball fights with Badger when snow was in the forecast.

The station's plans for Jenny involved much more than telling people whether or not to take umbrellas to work. They wanted a princess. Local news teams were small-town America's answer to royalty, they reasoned. Actually, they didn't reason it, as hardly anyone in television ever comes up with an idea independently. What they did was to go to a broadcasters' conference in Chicago, where they attended a seminar on "The Rating Value of News-Team Members as Community Celebrities."

The workshop speaker had, in fact, explained to the audience that media personalities performed the same functions in Middle America that the British royals did for the public in the United Kingdom. They lent their names to worthy causes, rode in parades, and served as figureheads and spokesmen for various civic projects. For the royal family, the rewards were an allowance from the civil list and a few castles to live in; for their American counterparts, it translated into ratings for the news-team celebrities' television station.

The Channel Four executives discussed this revelation on the plane back to Atlanta and they decided that of their four newspeople, perky blonde Jenny

Ramsay had the most potential for the role of community royal. She was wholesomely pretty rather than sexy, so that while men would find her attractive, women would still approve of her; she was young, inexperienced, and unmarried, which meant that her salary was not great, and her chances of relocating were small; and best of all, she was not terribly bright, which meant that she could discharge the endless social functions without going insane from boredom. Jenny Ramsay, the Weather Princess, was Channel Four's answer to prayer.

They sent her to Atlanta for two weeks of charm school, in which she learned to walk like a model, moderate her Southern accent for the benefit of a microphone, and to turn her best side toward the cameras. Her instructors brushed up her table manners, fashion sense, makeup skills, and posture. When Jenny Ramsay came back from Atlanta, she was not perfect, but after a few months' practice she acquired the polish to seem perfect. Although, as news anchor Victoria remarked privately, "The light in Jenny's eyes is the sun shining through the back of her head," most people were too dazzled to notice what a *dim* star she was.

The one thing that coaching had not taught Jenny Ramsay was the Manner. That she had learned on her own. It had not happened overnight, but gradually, Jenny had come to realize that all celebrities have a public persona as well as a private self. It isn't acting, exactly, and it isn't necessarily insincere; it's just a way of coping with strangers who expect to be treated like old pals.

After a few months of appearing on Channel Four, Jenny began to receive fan mail from people who obviously felt that she was one of the family. *We have dinner with you every night at 6:15*, one of them wrote. Strangers began to hail her by her first name in the supermarket, and people would stop her on the street and tell her long, pointless stories about themselves, or ask her personal questions, like whether she was married and what kind of car she drove. At first these intrusions were frightening to Jenny, because she thought that the intruders might be planning to kidnap her or drop in for breakfast or something equally repugnant. Finally she realized that people liked talking to her because she was famous, and that later they could recount their conversation with her to the guys at the office.

The station assigned her to be the March of Dimes chairman and the parade marshal. After they had her read children's letters to Santa Claus on the air and the newspaper pictured her cuddling the animal shelter's pet-of-the-week, she became the Patroness of the Valley. Thereafter, she could no more snub her constituents than Congressman Williams could.

By that time Jenny Ramsay had learned what the

public expected of her and she could give it graciously on an instant's notice. She called it Sparkle Plenty, after the character in the *Dick Tracy* comic strip. Sparkle Plenty meant that you smiled in public much more than anyone actually does and that you showed a degree of enthusiasm otherwise limited to two-year-olds and puppies. The voice, too, took on a quality of delight and emphasis that was quite absent from one's private conversations. When greeting her fans, she spoke in italics. *"How nice to mee-eet you! It is soo-oo sweet of you to say so! My autograph? Well, of cour-rse!"* Jenny had learned that if you didn't do that—if, in fact, you treated people as you normally treated your friends and family—they thought you were reserved or stuck up. But Sparkle Plenty was a very tiring activity. After a daylong broadcast from the county fair, Jenny found that her whole face ached from the muscle strain of constant smiling. Still, she was thoroughly proficient at it, and one always came away from an encounter with the Weather Princess feeling that one was her true friend, that she was "just like anybody else."

She wondered how she ought to act at Elizabeth MacPherson's wedding. Technically, of course, it was a private occasion, requiring the participation of the private Jenny Ramsay, and not the Channel Four Weather Princess, but lately it had seemed to her that she was recognized every time she went out in public, so that now she had to put on full makeup and dress clothes just to buy a quart of milk. Jenny was beginning to wonder if she could be Jenny Ramsay in any gathering at which strangers were present. She would have to see how it went.

A voice from the endless drone of the meeting interrupted her reverie. "What about you, Jenny? How do you feel about Dusty Miller?"

Jenny summoned a perky smile. "Great! My folks have a bunch of his records."

An instant later she remembered that this was a beautification meeting, and that Dusty Miller must be some kind of damned plant, but the committee members laughed merrily. Later they told people that Jenny Ramsay, while perfectly natural, was much wittier than she seemed on television.

◆　◆　◆

GEOFFREY TURNED off the Channel Four six o'clock news just as Jenny Ramsay was assuring a Stetson-wearing majorette that it would *not* rain on her parade. "I believe she is traveling in a mice-drawn pumpkin," he muttered. "How else could it take this long to get here from Virginia?"

"Antique shops," grunted Captain Grandfather from behind the pages of the *Chandler Grove Scout*. "Outlet malls. Even petting zoos. I think Elizabeth would stop to watch grass grow if somebody adver-tised it on a roadside billboard. Her mother's the same way."

"Well, if she doesn't get here soon, I shall be off to rehearsal," Geoffrey announced, in tones suggest-ing the magnitude of her loss.

"She'll probably wait up for you, Geoffrey. Keeping decent hours is something else she's not known for."

"I never could understand why early risers were so smug about it," said Geoffrey, for whom mornings were only an ugly rumor. "They go to bed at ten and get up at seven, and they act like they ought to get gold stars for doing it! That's nine hours sleep; while I, who go to bed at three A.M. or so, never get that much sleep. So, I ask you, who's the sloth?"

"You get more done if you get up with the chickens," said Captain Grandfather.

Geoffrey managed a frosty smile. "I much prefer owls. They're smarter."

The sound of a horn from the driveway diverted his attention from the argument. "About time!" he said, stalking out of the room.

Elizabeth's white hatchback was parked in the cir-cular driveway as close to the side door as she could manage. She was already hauling a collection of bags and parcels out of the backseat and stacking them on the concrete.

"Oh, good!" she cried, seeing Geoffrey approach.

"I was afraid I was going to have to carry all this by myself."

"What? No footmen?" Geoffrey inquired.

Elizabeth made a face at him. "You're going to be absolutely unbearable about all this, aren't you?"

"Oh, I don't know. Unbearable is such a subjective thing. I plan to enjoy myself hugely, though, which may prove annoying to you."

"I expect it will," said Elizabeth, handing him a totebag full of books. "You usually manage to make me feel like a perfect fool."

"When, alas, my goal is ever to prevent you from *being* one." He inspected the totebag and drew out the topmost book: *The Royal Wedding*. "Too late, I see!"

"I refuse to be cross with you, Geoffrey," said Elizabeth with a little laugh. "This is going to be the happiest day of my life."

"Yes," said Geoffrey. "I was afraid that it might." He flipped through the book, solemnly studying the color photographs of the glass coach, the sailor-suited page boys, and the red-liveried horsemen in the wedding procession. "And is this a portent of things to come? I'm afraid Chandler Grove doesn't run to landaus, but the high-school pep club could probably fix you up a float with some pastel toilet paper and twenty feet of chicken wire."

"I don't want a royal wedding," said Elizabeth between clenched teeth. "But I would like a lovely and memorable ceremony, since I *hope* to do this only once."

"Leave the bags here," said Geoffrey, setting the books down. "Let's go for a walk."

"Shouldn't I go in and say hello to everyone else?"

"They're watching *Jeopardy*," said Geoffrey. "You may as well wait until that's over if you want them to notice you. Come on."

Elizabeth looked for a long minute at the white castle across the road, and then with a little shudder she turned away. "All right," she said. "But let's not walk toward *that*."

"It is rather ominous, isn't it?" said Geoffrey. "I see it every day, and yet it still gives me chills. It's strange how you remember someone who has died violently, even if you weren't particularly fond of them."

Elizabeth nodded. "I know, but I truly don't want to think of him just now. Do you suppose that my coming here to have the wedding will bring back sad memories of Eileen?"

"Perhaps," said Geoffrey. "But at least you will be making new memories to overshadow the old ones. That may help."

They walked around to the back of the house, where a well-tended lawn gradually gave way to a field of tall grass that stretched a hundred yards or more to the edge of the woods.

◆

"It's so beautiful here," said Elizabeth, stopping to admire a bank of cabbage roses. "It makes the twentieth century seem far away."

"Well, it is," said Geoffrey. "Unfortunately, one must commute there."

"Yes. I don't know where *we're* going to live. It's very hard to manage with two careers."

"I should have thought that your two particular careers might make it easier than most," Geoffrey observed. "Obviously, he has to be near an ocean, on account of the seals, and you will find that there are dead bodies everywhere, so it shouldn't matter *where* you live."

Elizabeth frowned. "There's a bit more to it than that."

"Well, let's not get ahead of ourselves. First comes the wedding. Now, you are *sure* that you want to do this? Because I have seen you go off on some tangents that would make the *Flying Dutchman* seem carefully navigated."

"It isn't a whim," said Elizabeth softly.

"Well, I do rather like Cameron. He isn't the wet dishcloth you usually become enamored of. I suppose *he* knows what he's doing?"

"You will have to ask him," said Elizabeth dryly.

"And all this undue haste isn't *just* to meet the Queen? I have to tell you it sounds like a silly reason for getting married."

"You sound like Bill!" said Elizabeth, regarding Geoffrey with considerable surprise. "I haven't ever heard you sound so serious and responsible."

"I am Captain Grandfather's understudy," said Geoffrey with a grin. "Which you may take as a warning that you will probably be having this conversation again."

"Perhaps I should make an announcement," said Elizabeth. "This is not sudden and I am not impetuous. But the garden-party invitation is a great honor, and it seemed all right to rearrange our plans in view of it."

"You sound sane," said Geoffrey doubtfully. "But then so does Ernie Barlow when he talks about getting flying-saucer transmissions on his bridgework."

"It's going to be all right, Geoffrey," Elizabeth assured him. She played her trump card. "In fact, I was hoping that since you have such a wonderful sense of style, you might help me plan some of the arrangements for the wedding."

"We'll talk," said Geoffrey, looking smug. "I may have one or two little ideas."

Dearest Dawsons,

Wherever I wander (just now I'm in Rome),
Rest assured that you're thought of by your

GARDEN GNOME
Cheerie Bye!

◆   ◆   ◆

CHAPTER

7

CLARINE MASON didn't feel like dusting her husband Emmet's picture. She didn't feel like dusting Emmet, either.

Her feet were tired, her back ached, and she was positive she was coming down with a cold. She tossed her feather duster onto the glass-topped coffee table and plopped down on the sofa. Living by yourself didn't make the work *that* much easier, not in a big old farmhouse like this one—Emmet's family homestead, one of the original houses in the community of

Chandler Grove. Trust him to stick her with a barn like this. Sure, she could skimp on the cooking and serve leftovers three times running, but the house got dusty just as fast, and now she had Emmet's chores to do as well as her own. There was an acre of yard to mow, and screens to patch, and the back-porch steps needed fixing. Why, it would have been a load of work for a woman half her age. When folks at church asked her if she missed Emmet, the very thought of all those extra chores brought tears to her eyes, and she could say with perfect sincerity, "Oh, I do miss him! More than ever!"

The tin roof would need painting before winter.

Clarine cast a sour look at the smiling features of Emmet J. Mason, neatly encased in an art nouveau silver frame on the mantelpiece. People used to say he looked like Conway Twitty, which Emmet used to take as a compliment. The country singer and Emmet both had blue-black hair that they wore fluffed up like cotton candy, and they had beefy faces with little round eyes that shone with the sincerity of a snake-oil preacher. A lot Emmet cared about the chores or the state of her health. When had he ever cared about anything but his crazy obsession?

Well, there *had* been a time when Emmet had been interested in her and in his hometown, but years of exasperation had obscured those pleasant memories, replacing them with half-remembered quarrels and with the numbness that set in when nothing Emmet said or did mattered to her anymore. Clarine tried to remember the Emmet she'd married in 1958; maybe she ought to put his high-school photo on the mantelpiece instead of the later one. He'd seemed like such a nice, steady boy in those days. He had played high-school varsity football, which had impressed the shy sophomore Clarine, and he'd worked weekends in his father's hardware store. It was understood that he was going to take over the business one day.

She had got engaged to him at seventeen, when he went in the army, and she'd written him letters on pink stationery the whole time he was stationed in Germany. Emmet did take over Mason's Hardware in 1976, when Daddy Earl had his stroke, but by then he had lost interest in the commercial possibilities in Chandler Grove, Georgia.

"Let's sell the store and go to California!" he'd say.

Clarine said she hadn't lost a thing in the state of California.

"Life's just passing me by here in the sticks!" Emmet would sigh. "I know I could make it as an actor."

Emmet had played the role of Emily's father in the Chandler Grove production of *Our Town*; the Scout reviewer had pronounced him "adequate." The senior English class, following the play in their literature books with tiny flashlights, claimed he hadn't missed a line.

Emmet followed up that success with a portrayal of James Oglethorpe, founder of the colony of Georgia, in the town pageant. After that, he figured the only thing keeping him out of the movies was geographical inconvenience.

Clarine said relocating was out of the question because she didn't want to star in a real-life documentary about damn-fool Georgians caught in a California earthquake that they hadn't ought to be in. And besides, there was her mother to think of, past seventy and suffering from arthritis. No, Clarine insisted, there were too many family obligations—not to mention the Mason family business—to keep them in Chandler Grove, and she wasn't going to see Emmet throw it all away trying to become another Bob Eubanks.

She had been right, too, she thought, scowling at Emmet's smarmy Kodachrome smile. *Stay home*, she'd said. *You're not slick enough for California.* But talking to Emmet about show business was like Emily trying to talk to her folks in Act Three of *Our Town*: she just couldn't make herself heard. In the end, Emmet trumped up a business trip to California for a hardware convention, and he announced that he was staying an extra three days to talk to some Hollywood agents.

Look what had come of that.

The day before Emmet was due back, Clarine received a phone call from the California Highway Patrol, telling her that Emmet had been killed in a car wreck on the Ventura Freeway. The accident had been so bad that the car caught fire, the officer told her. There wasn't much left of Emmet J. Mason. Did she want him cremated?

Before she thought about it, Clarine blurted out, "You might as well. A little more heat won't matter to Emmet at this point."

So they had. A couple of days after the phone call, the UPS truck had pulled up in the yard and the man made her sign for a heavy package, about the size of a shoe box, wrapped in brown paper. When Clarine took it in the house and unwrapped it, she found a blue-flowered ginger jar with a note attached that said: *Enclosed are the remains of Emmet J. Mason. With our deepest sympathy*, and signed by some California funeral director.

Clarine put Emmet on the mantelpiece between the carved-oak rooster clock and the silver-framed photograph. For a long time she was too shocked to feel much of anything, except an occasional flare of anger when she looked at the jar. Gradually she came to realize that Emmet had probably died happy, pursuing his silly fantasy of stardom, and that she didn't miss him all that much. So she sold the hardware store, banked the life-insurance money, and lived as frugally as she could, because she didn't want to run out of money in her old age. She'd never had a job in her life; couldn't even balance a checkbook till Emmet's death forced her to learn. She didn't want to have to clean other people's houses for slave wages when she was old and feeble, so she did all the chores herself, and she watched every penny.

She was about to get up and dust the mantelpiece when the telephone rang. Clarine hurried out into the hall and got it by the third ring. "Hello?"

"Mrs. Mason," said an unfamiliar voice, notably lacking a Southern accent.

"Yes," she said warily, ready to slam down the receiver at the first sign of a sales pitch.

"Wife of Emmet J. Mason?" he continued.

"Yes." She didn't bother to correct him. Best not to let strangers know you lived alone. Maybe she'd won a sweepstakes, she thought.

"This is Sergeant Gene Vega of the California Highway Patrol. I'm sorry to have to tell you that your husband Emmet J. Mason was killed in an auto accident here this morning. . . ."

"What, *again?*"

◆　◆　◆

SHERIFF WESLEY Rountree was reading this week's edition of the *Chandler Grove Scout*, an activity that never took as long as his coffee break. The front page was good for about three minutes, if you read slowly, and generally consisted of one city government story, one wreck or weather story, and a heartwarming human interest piece featuring either kids or old ladies. After that came the community news, devoted to toddlers' birthday parties or visits from out-of-state relatives. Then came the local grocery ads, accompanied by a few freebie news releases from the U.S. Department of Agriculture (THE GYPSY MOTH IS NOT YOUR FRIEND) and a page of high-school sports stories that contrived to mention the name of every conceivable person present at the event (*After the third inning, Cheerleader Mascot Shannon Gentry waved to her grandmother, Mrs. Lois Andrews*).

Wesley glanced at his coffee cup. It was nearly full, and he was already past the high point of the issue: the irate letter to the editor from Mr. Julian, the local curmudgeon.

Deputy Clay Taylor, on the other hand, was already on his second cup of herbal tea, deeply immersed in a crime novel. He was hunched over his desk, his rimless glasses teetering midway down his nose, lips pursed, as he turned the page of the thick paperback entitled *Sergeant Luger: Crack Shot*. Wesley was surprised at his deputy's choice of reading matter. Usually the Peace Corps veteran restricted his leisure study to socially significant works like *The Coalition for Central American Rights Newsletter* or pamphlets by groups with names like Defenders of the Ozone. Just bringing Clay's mail back from the post office box

◆

could raise your social consciousness, the sheriff contended.

Wesley turned a page of the newspaper. "I see where the Chandlers' niece is getting married," he remarked. "I think we met her during the Chandler case, didn't we? The one that kinda resembled Linda Ronstadt."

Clay Taylor refused to rise to the conversational bait. He turned another page.

"Says here she's studying forensic anthropology in graduate school. I used to think that meant analyzing the way different cultures talked, because back when I was in high school, speech class was called forensics. Turns out it means analyzing human remains. Interesting sort of job."

With an absent nod in the direction of his boss, the deputy turned another page.

He must have reached a sex scene, thought Wesley, returning to his own choice of reading matter. He scanned the rest of the page and caught sight of a familiar name. "Well, Clay, looks like you got mentioned in the *Scout* this week," he called out.

The reply was a grunt from behind the cover of *Sergeant Luger: Crack Shot*.

"No picture, though. Marshal Pavlock has written up the Halliburtons' account of how they called you to save them from the wild animal in their cellar. Listen here: *A feral whine was coming from the darkness of* the Halliburtons' basement, and upon discovering that the basement light had burned out after being accidentally left on, Bryan Halliburton declined to descend into the basement armed with only a flashlight to confront the beast. They thought that it might be a wildcat, using their premises for its den, and they decided to appeal for help to the local sheriff's department. Enter the intrepid deputy T. Clay Taylor."

With a weary sigh, the aforementioned intrepid deputy marked his place in his novel with a parking ticket and listened to Wesley's dramatic reading. "I wish he hadn't run that story," he said.

Wesley chuckled. "Why not? It's a corker. *Deputy Taylor did not draw his gun as he crept slowly down the concrete steps toward the Halliburtons' washing machine. He heard the menacing noise they had told him about. It was then that he informed them that bloodshed would not be called for.*" The sheriff rattled the paper, too overcome to continue.

"*All they had to do was change the battery on their smoke alarm and the noise would stop,*" said Clay, supplying the story's punch line. He shrugged. "Can I go back to my book now?"

Wesley took a sobering sip of black coffee. "What do you want to read that thing for anyhow?" he asked.

"It's a modern parable of good and evil, full of riveting authenticity about the deadly game in the inner cities," said Clay, consulting the back cover for blurbs.

"Oh crap," said the sheriff. "It's a male romance novel is what it is."

"It's reality," said Clay, looking earnest as usual.

"*This* is reality!" said Wesley, waving the *Chandler Grove Scout*. "Killer smoke alarms. Two years without firing a shot in the line of duty. That thing you've got is what a lot of humorless people *hope* is reality. Because if the world is grim and sordid, then it means they're not missing anything."

Clay Taylor shrugged. It wasn't easy working with an incurable optimist when the world was going to hell in a Central American handbasket. When the phone rang a few moments later, he found himself wishing that it would be someone reporting an axe murder. That would show Wesley.

◆ ◆ ◆

AMANDA CHANDLER downed the last of her grapefruit juice with an expression suggesting that she would refuse the offer of an antidote. Normally, she had orange juice, hot chocolate, and sweet rolls for breakfast, but an unhappy interview with her dressmaker the week before had changed her regimen. She would *not* wear an empire waist to "hide her tummy," and that was that. Perhaps no one else at the wedding would know her dress size, but *she* would. A new note of austerity crept into the menus at Long Meadow Farm, prompting Geoffrey to inquire if this was the anniversary of the Bataan Death March. Amanda was not amused.

"I have to go and get my hair done this morning, Elizabeth," she announced, frowning at her niece's plate of bacon and eggs. "I have asked the caterer to stop by this morning, and I shall leave that detail of the wedding to you." Her tone suggested that the mere discussion of petits fours and pound cake could be fattening.

Elizabeth took a swallow of black coffee. "All right, Aunt Amanda," she said meekly. "Is there anything in particular that I should ask for?"

The words *melba toast* hovered on Amanda Chandler's lips, but she said, "Draw up a list of things you like, and ask if they can do them, and for how much. If that doesn't work, see what they recommend. I will, of course, check with you when I return." *And change everything to suit myself* was the unspoken message.

"Who are the caterers?" asked Elizabeth as an afterthought. "Anyone I know?"

"No. They are a new business. I haven't used them before, either. They are called Earthling. Charles recommended them."

As a reflex, Elizabeth looked around for her cousin, but Charles was gone, of course. With the wedding frenzy increasing exponentially by the hour, the Chandler men had taken to fleeing the house as early as possible each morning to avoid the day's disruptions.

Even Geoffrey, who normally kept bat's hours, managed to wrest himself out of the house and down to the community playhouse before nine.

"I will be back in time for lunch," said Amanda, who was changing from her reading glasses to her driving glasses. "Will you be here?"

"No. I promised Jenny Ramsay that I'd meet her for lunch." Seeing her aunt's look of stone-faced resignation, she added, "I'm having a salad."

"Right. I'll be off then. You might make a list of questions for the caterer while you wait. Goodbye."

Elizabeth found a notepad beside the telephone. She wandered off into the parlor, muttering, "Carrot sticks . . . cheese cubes . . . onion dip . . ." The prospect of interviewing a caterer made her uneasy. The word conjured up visions of a heavyset older man with an Olivier accent with a rosebud in his lapel. And he would know what kind of rose it was. Elizabeth shuddered, knowing that she was not equal to the task of directing such a being.

Her list was going badly. She had changed the flavor of the wedding cake six times—mostly from chocolate to something else and back again—when she heard the doorbell chime. "Why am I so nervous?" said Elizabeth as she walked toward the door. "I'm sure he'll be very polite—in a condescending sort of way."

Summoning her brightest smile, she flung open the door. "Good morning!" she called out. "I am the bride."

"Far out," said the visitor.

Elizabeth stared at the apparition on Aunt Amanda's personalized Orvis doormat. It was a gaunt, bearded man in his late thirties (or forties, or fifties). He was the type that made it difficult to tell. He reminded her of somebody—matted black hair, gaunt triangular face, and burning black eyes. A photograph from her world history book back in high school. She had it now! Idly, she wondered what he was doing on her doorstep in thongs and a Rainbow Sweat Lodge T-shirt.

"Er-uh?" said Elizabeth, trying to adjust to the fact that the Admirable Crichton she had been expecting had defaulted in favor of the mad monk Rasputin. She was trying frantically to invent conversation, but nothing in English or Russian or even sign language occurred to her.

"You called for a caterer?"

Elizabeth's eyes widened, but she managed to say, "Yes, of course. And you must be the director of Earthling."

He shrugged. "I'm one of the group. Anybody who'd claim to be the head of the company would have to be on some kind of domination trip, and I'm not into that, but, yeah, I'm the caterer you asked for."

"I'm Elizabeth MacPherson. Won't you come in, Mr.—"

"Josh."

"Come in, Josh."

"Actually, that's my last name," he said, strolling into the newly waxed front hall. "Some of the members of our New Age community decided to adopt Indian names a few years back to show solidarity with the people of Bhopal, and I changed mine to Rogan Josh, because I'd seen it written somewhere. After I found out what it meant, I was going to change it, but everybody said that that would be an act of unspiritual arrogance, so I kept it. You can call me R.J."

"What does it mean?"

He frowned. "It's a menu item in Indian restaurants. Spiced lamb."

Elizabeth nodded with what she hoped was polite interest. "I have this list," she said.

"List?" He was looking around the living room.

"Yes, of some things I thought we'd have at the reception. Won't you sit down?" She motioned him to the velvet love seat, and retrieved her notepad of scribbles and crossed-out items. "I'm afraid it's hard to decipher. I changed my mind several times. Maybe I'd better read it to you."

R.J. leaned back in a pose of studied meditation: eyes closed, head thrown back. He signaled for her to begin.

"Carrot sticks," said Elizabeth. "I mean, I thought we ought to have a relish tray so that people could nibble fresh vegetables, perhaps with a dip alongside it. You know—celery, bell-pepper strips, broccoli . . ."

R.J. opened his eyes. "No broccoli."

Elizabeth hesitated. "Why? Isn't it in season?"

"Doesn't matter," he told her, sitting up again and peering at her list. "Broccoli is imported—" He paused for effect. "From *Guatemala.*"

"Oh. Well, I'm sure we can afford—"

"Guatemala has one of the most repressive and brutal military regimes in the world. By buying their agricultural products—"

"Okay! Forget the broccoli," said Elizabeth quickly. She consulted her list. "Little sandwiches, cheese puffs, mints, coffee . . ."

R.J. looked grim. "Coffee," he announced, "is sprayed with a number of pesticides that are considered too dangerous for use in the United States."

Elizabeth glared at him. "We'll take our chances."

"That's not the point. The workers who *grow* the coffee are endangered by the use of these compounds, and so are the animal species which make their homes—"

"I want coffee!"

"I guess we could buy Nicaraguan coffee," R.J. conceded. "They have the strictest pesticide laws in Central America. Fruit juice is healthier, though."

"Fine. We'll have an orange-juice punch."

"Florida orange juice, of course. The South American stuff comes from land that was previously either rain forest or was being used by small farmers to grow subsistence crops to feed their families."

Elizabeth took a deep breath. "Look," she said, "do you do much business in catering?"

R.J. shrugged. "Sure. We did the Summer Solstice Meditation Retreat and the Crystal Channeling Workshop, and we always do the beans-and-rice fund-raisers for the Central American Prayer and Protest Group. You want references?"

"No, thank you," said Elizabeth, standing up to indicate that the interview was over. "I'll be in touch."

"We also have a minister," R.J. offered, "In case you want to be married for more than one incarnation."

"Thanks," said Elizabeth. "I'll keep it in mind."

◆　◆　◆

WESLEY ROUNTREE left his deputy in charge of the office while he went out to talk to Clarine Mason. He wasn't sure what sort of crime was involved here, but whatever it was seemed to be going on in California, and Wesley was sure that he could manage Clarine, hysterics and all.

When he got to the old white house on Mason Cove Road, he found Clarine waiting for him at the gate, but the hysterics were not in evidence.

"Stupidest damned thing I ever heard of!" she fumed, when he was within hailing distance.

"Well, it does seem strange," said Wesley in the mild, amiable tone he used for domestic-violence cases, mental patients, and local politicians. "Why don't we go in, and you tell me about it right from the beginning, and I'll make notes."

Clarine did not budge from the gate. "Wesley, if I'd wanted to be interviewed, I'd have called the *National Enquirer*. What I want is some *action*."

The sheriff sighed. "I'll do everything I can, Clarine, but first I have to get it to make sense to me."

She pushed open the gate and motioned for Wesley to follow. "I can fix you some iced tea," she said in a belated attempt at hospitality. "And I made some zucchini bread."

Wesley accepted both offers, telling himself that fixing the food would help to calm the witness. Besides, with his job you never knew when you were going to miss a meal. When he was settled in the green velvet armchair, balancing a dessert plate of cake on his knee, Clarine sat down on the sofa facing him and began her story.

"It looks like I am Emmet Mason's wife twice removed," she remarked.

"Now, I know Emmet was killed on a trip to California. Was it five years ago?"

His widow nodded. "That's when he went out there,

anyhow. And I got this call from the highway patrol, saying that Emmet had been killed in a car wreck in Los Angeles, which I did not find difficult to believe, considering what I've heard about the way they drive out there."

Wesley set down his iced tea and scribbled a few notes. "Okay. Do you remember the officer's name?"

Clarine sighed at the stupidity of the question. "The content of the phone call—him telling me that my husband was dead—registered considerably more than the details of the caller."

"Had to ask," said Wesley, waving for her to continue.

"Well, the officer—whoever he was—said that Emmet had been burned beyond recognition, that he'd have to be cremated, and that they would send him back."

"What about insurance?"

"They said they'd send a death certificate, and they did. That's all Bob Barclay down at Georgia Colonial Health wanted to see. And, of course, the newspaper here did a nice write-up about Emmet, with a photo of him from *Our Town*, and I enclosed that, too."

"All I know is what I read in the papers," muttered Wesley, scribbling again. "So they sent the death certificate—and Emmet—back to you in the mail?"

"UPS," said Clarine. "Of course, my first impulse was to go to California, and I said so to the officer on the phone, but he said, 'What for?' And I had to admit he had me there. It wasn't like I could do anything out there. Emmet was already dead, and we didn't know a soul west of Oklahoma. So when he offered to ship the remains back to Georgia, I said fine."

"So by and by this package arrives, containing an urn and a death certificate."

"Right. Now, Wesley, I just know that the next thing out of your mouth is going to be to ask me did I keep the wrapping off the package, and the answer is no. But the vase is right up there on the mantel."

Wesley Rountree looked up at the urn in the center of the mantle. It was dark blue cloisonné, in the shape of a ginger jar, and it was about eight inches high. *Exhibit A*, thought Wesley. "And he's in there?"

"*Something's* in there," snapped Clarine. "I never opened the lid to examine the contents."

"I reckon I will." The sheriff sighed, starting to get up.

"Not here."

"Oh, no. I understand about your feelings toward the deceased and all—"

"I just vacuumed," said Clarine.

◆　◆　◆

THE FOXCROFT INN in Milton's Forge had been Elizabeth's choice of a restaurant for lunch with Jenny.

Although she had never been there, she remembered newspaper ads, showing the old half-timbered building with its inn sign reminiscent of a British pub, and mentioning its Olde Worlde cuisine. It had once been a frontier tavern, back in the days when the hills of Georgia were considered The West. Elizabeth thought that this blend of style and tradition would make a suitable setting for an occasion so momentous as a luncheon with one's maid of honor.

She parked in the gravel lot that had been laid between the inn and the old stables, then went around to the iron-hinged front door in search of Jenny. *I wish I had watched the eleven o'clock news last night*, thought Elizabeth. *What if I don't recognize her?*

As it happened, recognizing Jenny Ramsay was not a problem, once Elizabeth was able to catch a glimpse of her within the knot of people surrounding her. The smiling blonde in a confection of pink resembled Elizabeth's high-school friend in the same way that the picture of a rose in a plant catalogue resembles the actual flower in your ill-tended garden. Elizabeth looked at the pink linen suit and then at her own khaki skirt and scoop-neck T-shirt and then back at the vision of loveliness who was now signing an autograph for a man in a three-piece suit. It was going to be a long lunch.

"Reservation for two for lunch," she said when the hostess finally noticed her. "MacPherson."

"Okay," said the hostess, consulting her list. "It could be a few minutes. We're pretty busy. Is the other party here yet?"

Solemnly Elizabeth pointed to the crowd. "I'm having lunch with Jenny Ramsay."

"Oh! Well, I'll show you to your table whenever she's ready, ma'am."

◆　◆　◆

SINCE CLAY WAS no longer reading *Sergeant Luger: Crack Shot* when the sheriff returned, he assumed that it had been a slow afternoon at the office. "I'm back," he announced, checking his desk for notes. Not finding any, he cleared off a spot near the pencil mug and set down a blue cloisonné urn.

"No messages?"

"Not a thing. Hill-Bear came in a little while ago. He's out on patrol now."

Hill-Bear Melkerson, the other deputy, was a human St. Bernard who made up in enthusiasm what he lacked in intellect. His name was actually Hilbert, but he had changed it permanently to Hill-Bear after his high-school French teacher informed him that this was its correct pronunciation. Hill-Bear was excellent at crowd control, good at breaking up fights, and passable as a traffic patrolman, but he could never be an investigator. Wesley planned to assign Clay to assist him on the Mason case while Hill-Bear attended to the normal routine.

"Finished the book, did you?" asked Wesley.

Clay shrugged. "I just skim 'em. Nice vase. You decorating the office now?"

"No. This is evidence. I want it photographed, fingerprinted, and anything else you can think of to do to it, short of opening it."

"Is that from the Mason place? What's going on out there?"

Wesley shook his head. "It's a new one on me, that's for sure. You remember when Emmet died, out there in California?"

"Vaguely."

"About five years ago. Clarine gets a phone call telling her about the wreck. Then she gets a package containing this urn and a death certificate. I brought it along, too."

"Fingerprints and photos, too? Okay. So, as far as Chandler Grove is concerned, Emmet is history, right? And then today Mrs. Mason gets *another* call from California telling her that her husband is dead?"

"Right. But this time she has more presence of mind. She writes down the officer's name and the phone number. L.A. area code: 213. I got it here. Gene Vega. And she gets details about the accident."

"Was it the same as before? Burned beyond recognition?"

"No. I called them back while I was out at Clarine's place. She insisted. Wanted to get it straight as soon as possible. I got Sergeant Vega and, sure enough, he's a real California police officer. Seemed kind of put out that we doubted him, but then I explained that we'd been through this before. He grumped a bit about clerical irregularities, but said he'd check."

"Everything's on computer out there," said Clay.

Wesley made a face. "Thank *you*, Sergeant Luger. I know that. Anyway, he hit a few keys and told me that they had no record of an earlier demise of Emmet Mason of Chandler Grove, Georgia, in a wreck or any other way, but he was here to tell me that the present Emmet Mason was deader'n a mackerel in the L.A. morgue. I thought I might have to go out and see about it, but what do you reckon he said then?"

"Fax, of course," said Clay, looking bored.

The sheriff sighed. "I hate a know-it-all. But, yes, he said that in view of our limited technology here— on account of the county commissioners' views on budget deficits—that he couldn't use the machine they normally use to transmit data from one police department to another. But he said that they would take a picture of the corpse and fax it to us here in Georgia, and we'd see if it was all a big mistake."

"We don't have a fax machine, either," Clay pointed out.

"No," said Wesley, "But we will have when I tell

the commissioners that they are laughing at us in California. Meanwhile, I scouted up a machine on my second try, and he's sending it there."

The deputy thought hard. "Newspaper office?"

"And let Marshall get wind of this? He was my last resort. I was going for confidentiality."

"The florist shop!" cried Clay. "No," he said, thinking better of it. "You said *confidentiality*, and there's no way that Lucy—"

Wesley scowled. "I swore her to secrecy."

Clay kept a straight face. "Uh-huh." He nodded toward the blue urn on the sheriff's desk. "And when are you going to open that?"

"I hope I don't have to," said Wesley.

◆　◆　◆

"IT'S SO GOOD TO see you again!" said Jenny Ramsay, still with a hint of italics in her voice. "And just think! You're getting *married*. Isn't that exciting!"

Elizabeth smiled. "You seem to be having a pretty exciting time of it yourself, Jen."

Jenny rolled her eyes. "Isn't it *silly?*" She giggled. "It's just part of the job, though."

"It seems very strange for someone who's supposed to be responsible for weather."

"The station feels that the news team should serve as community leaders," said Jenny. "So I do a lot of charity work and public appearances, and people seem to think they know me—because they watch me on TV every day."

"I see."

"Anyway, I think a lot of people are very lonely," Jenny said, lapsing into her broadcaster-sincere tone. "When I attend one of these public events, I try to be as kind and gracious as I can, and to—you know—say something *meaningful*, because I know that some of those people will treasure what I have to say for the rest of their lives."

"Well, how are things going with *you?*" asked Elizabeth. "I mean, besides the job. Are you seeing anybody?"

Jenny shook her head. "I have so many commitments to worthy civic projects that I hardly have time to do my laundry." She laughed merrily. "But of course I do. My laundry, I mean. I just love the smell of clean sheets, don't you?"

Elizabeth noticed a waitress hovering at Jenny's elbow. "I think she wants us to order."

The waitress blushed to the ruffle on her Martha Washington cap. "Oh, yes, ma'am! I'll take your order if you're ready, but I was wondering if Miss Ramsay would sign my pad here?"

Jenny opened her purse and pulled out a postcard with her photograph on it. "If you'd like to have one of these . . ."

"Oh, could I? Would you make it out to Kimberly?"

"Of course, Kimberly. How do you spell that?"

Elizabeth retreated behind her menu while this transaction took place, surfacing only long enough to order a chef salad and iced tea for lunch. Jenny asked for crabmeat salad and a white-wine spritzer.

"I'm sorry about the interruption," whispered Jenny when the waitress had left. "I'm used to it by now, but I realize that it must seem strange to you."

"I don't mind," said Elizabeth. "I'm glad that things are going well for you. I remember when your major role model was a television genie."

Jenny made a face. "And now I am one!" She laughed. "Okay! That's enough shoptalk. Now tell me all about this fiancé of yours!"

Elizabeth spent a happy ten minutes discussing Cameron Dawson and then went into detail about the wedding plans. Jenny toyed with her salad and nodded encouragingly.

"And the best part," said Elizabeth, "is that we are invited to the Royal Garden Party in Edinburgh, and I will get to see the Queen!"

"Really!" cooed Jenny.

"Oh, not that we'll actually have tea with the Queen, of course," said Elizabeth, feeling that modesty was in order. "Thousands of people are invited to the garden party. Everybody queues up on the lawn of the palace of Holyroodhouse, and they have their tea standing up, while the Queen and her attendants take tea in a little tent in sight of the crowd."

Jenny wrinkled her nose. "Poor dear."

"No," said Elizabeth. "It's an honor to be invited."

"I meant the Queen," said Jenny. "I know *exactly* how she feels. Every year the station has a Fourth of July picnic and people sit in the park with their little sandwiches and *watch* while we eat lunch in our marquees. And do you know the first thing Badger and I do when the picnic is over? We go out to *lunch*, because you can't really eat anything with four thousand people staring at you every minute."

"I suppose not," said Elizabeth with a little laugh. She indicated her own half-eaten salad. "It's hard to eat when you're contemplating being the center of attention at a formal wedding, too!"

Jenny studied her carefully. "Well, I'm sure you'll benefit from the fast," she said judiciously. "Are you in an exercise program?"

Elizabeth was saved from a reply by the approach of a silver-haired lady who wanted to know if Miss Ramsay would autograph her napkin.

◆ ◆ ◆

CAMERON DAWSON, wearing an ancient navy guernsey and needlecord jeans, was changing the air filter on the family Micra. He liked to accomplish these little tasks when he was at home because Ian was hopeless as a handyman and their mother never got around to seeing that anyone professional undertook the maintenance of the car—or the plumbing or the boiler. Cameron's first chore upon arriving for a visit was to determine what was leaking, malfunctioning, or needed cleaning. He then set aside a portion of each day to put everything right again.

The air filter looked as if it had been rolled down a chimney. Cameron frowned, making a mental note to draw up a schedule of when things ought to be done for the car. Now that he was working outside the U.K., he couldn't be sure of getting home often enough to keep the car from being destroyed by neglect. He must impress on them the need for regular upkeep. While he was about it, perhaps he ought to find an honest mechanic. Preferably someone who made house calls.

"Here you are," said Ian, wheeling his bicycle in and propping it against the wall by the tool bench. "I went into the house just now, but no one was about. I might have known I'd find you here. Busy?"

"Obviously," snapped Cameron. "I would have a good deal more leisure if you would learn how to take care of things around here."

"Probably not," said Ian cheerfully. "I expect I'd only render them unfixable. Machines seem to sense that I am afraid of them. It makes them hostile. I thought I'd let you know that the afternoon post has arrived."

The only reply was a grunt from beneath the hood of the Micra.

"Seeing how you carried on so the last time you didn't get a letter the instant it got here, I thought I would hunt you up and notify you this time. Sorry I couldn't manage a fanfare of trumpets."

Cameron, with a smudge of grease on one cheek, emerged from the depths of the engine and leaned against the wing (known to Elizabeth as the fender). "Well? Did I get anything?"

"A package from your betrothed. The customs form says *Invitations*, so I have taken care to make plans for this evening. You may address them yourself, and good luck to you. I can let you have some stamps, though, at a price."

Cameron sighed. He had finished the air filter and was now cleaning spark plugs. "Anything else?" he called out.

"Letter from the Queen, by the look of it. Royal seal and all. You'd better wash your hands before I give it to you."

"Read it to me."

"Hold on. Let me set the rest of this stuff down. I wouldn't want to tear the letter, in case you want to frame it." He slit the envelope carefully with his penknife. "Just another invitation to the garden party.

This one is to Dr. and *Mrs.* Cameron Dawson. So that's all right. Elizabeth can rest easy now. It has a funny sound to it, doesn't it?"

"What?"

"Dr. and Mrs. Makes you seem quite old, somehow."

Cameron nodded. "I know what you mean. Well, I'll have to call Elizabeth and tell her the good news. Really, though, I don't think she ever doubted that she'd be allowed to attend."

"Touching faith in authority, that. Oh, by the way, we did get one more piece of mail."

"Yes?"

"Postcard from the gnome."

Cameron left the car and went to see for himself. "Bloody hell!" He grinned. "Not another one! Where is he this time?"

Ian held out the card. "Alaska."

"Not—"

"I'm afraid so. *Nome.*"

The front of the card bore the word *Alaska* in large red letters and pictured a team of grinning huskies pulling a sled. Cameron flipped the card over and read the inscription: *To boldly go where Gnome man has gone before.*

CHAPTER

8

WESLEY ROUNTREE WAS wedged into the corner of the back room of Lucy's Country Garden Flower Shop, trying not to bump into the shelf of bud vases situated perilously close to his left shoulder. On the table in front of him was a fax machine, being attended by Lucy herself, who looked as solemn as a death-row chaplain.

"I have to warn you, Wesley," she whispered. "This machine doesn't do too good on photographs. It's mainly for transmitting paperwork, and it keeps you from having to be on the phone all the time. But don't expect the picture to come out looking all that great."

The sheriff sighed. "It probably wouldn't, anyway." He sighed. "With Emmet being dead and all."

"Well, I just wanted to warn you," said Lucy, straightening her pink smock with an air of one who has done her duty. "I hope you can tell if it's him or not."

Clay Taylor, lounging in the curtained doorway, held up Clarine Mason's photograph of her late husband. "We can compare it to this," he said. "It'll give us something to go on."

"And please, Lucy," said Wesley, "don't go spreading news about this around town. We don't know that there's any crime at all connected with this. It's probably some mistaken-identity business, and I'd hate to get Clarine all upset with rumors."

Lucy was a picture of injured innocence. "If you don't trust me, Wesley, you could have gone to the highway patrol at Milton's Forge and used whatever it is the police are *supposed* to use."

"Officer Vega is sending me a copy of the picture and a set of fingerprints, Lucy. Second-day air. I just wanted a general idea of what the fellow looked like."

Lucy glanced at the photograph in the deputy's hand. "Well, if Conway Twitty has gone and died on the L.A. Freeway, you will be none the wiser," she sniffed.

The machine beeped, then clicked into action, commanding their immediate attention.

"I hope it's not another flower order," muttered Clay.

The florist glared at him. "Thanks a lot!"

"No," said Wesley, peering at the edge of the paper emerging from the machine. "It says *Los Angeles* at the top. We'll know in a minute here."

They waited in silence while the machine thermo-printed the message from California. When it had finished, Wesley eased the sheet of paper out of the machine and motioned for Clay to bring the photograph. Officer Vega had sent them a copy of the black-and-white Polaroid photo of the deceased and a photocopy of a California driver's license identifying the man as Emmet J. Mason.

Wesley squinted at the photo. Since shades of gray do not transmit in fax communications, the image was a stark contrast of black and white, omitting age lines and other details that might have helped in the identification process. He set the picture down beside the framed photo of Emmet Mason. He looked from one to the other.

"It's hard to say, isn't it?"

Lucy tossed her head. "I told you about sending pictures!" she sniffed.

"There's a definite resemblance," said Clay. "And the ears are the same shape. They always say that's a big tip-off in identifying people."

The sheriff nodded. "I'd say the likeness is good enough to justify me asking a few more questions, even before we get the official photo." He turned to the florist with his most disarming smile. "Lucy, I thank you for your hospitality. And I sure do appreciate your discretion. When I get ready to donate some flowers to the church in honor of my parents' anniversary, I'll give you a call."

When they were outside, Clay asked, "What do you reckon this means?"

Wesley sighed. "I'd say it means that reports of Emmet Mason's death were a trifle premature. And I reckon I have to drive back out there and tell Clarine that she's a widow."

"That won't be news."

"No, but it won't be pleasant, either. Damn that Emmet! I wonder what he was about."

"That's not the half of it," grunted Clay. "I wonder who's in that urn on your desk."

ELIZABETH MACPHERSON was curled up on the chintz sofa in the den, reading a hymnbook. "It's so difficult to decide what music to choose," she said, running her finger down the list of titles. "I wonder what they play for weddings in Scotland."

"'Amazing Grace,'" said Geoffrey. "Though it's considered bad form to use it if that happens to be the bride's name."

"I think 'Greensleeves' is a very nice tune," she mused.

Geoffrey looked up from his playscript of *Twelfth Night*. "Since the other title of that melody is 'What Child Is This,' I implore you not to use it. You know how people jump to conclusions. What else are you considering?"

"I have a list of songs that were used at some of the royal weddings," she said, picking up another book. "Prince Charles and Princess Diana had 'I Vow to Thee My Country.'"

"Very appropriate for them, Elizabeth, but in this case it rather implies that you are handing Georgia over to the Redcoats."

Elizabeth scowled. "That was several wars ago."

"It would be worse if you were marrying a Yankee," Geoffrey conceded, "but I advise you to abandon the idea all the same. What are the other choices?"

"'O Perfect Love.'"

"Not bad. Who used that one?"

"The Duke and Duchess of Windsor." She sighed. "Oh, dear, I wouldn't like to identify with *her* on my wedding day, poor thing. She'd had two husbands before Edward. Her husband's family hated her. Her mother-in-law Queen Mary never spoke to her." Elizabeth shuddered. "And everybody blamed her for the King's abdication."

"Cameron is not required to give up seals or porpoises on your account, I trust?"

"No. And everybody seems very calm about the prospect of our marriage. Congratulations, but no confetti, if you know what I mean. Not wildly ecstatic."

"You're thinking of Princess Diana, I suppose? I've always thought that Prince Charles would have been driven to marry her by public and family opinion alone."

"No. Actually I was thinking of Charles's grandmother, Elizabeth of York. The Queen Mum. She was old Queen Mary's *other* daughter-in-law. There was no way poor divorced American Wallis could compete with *her*. Of course, she had a better pedigree than Wallis Simpson. When the future George VI proposed to her, she was the daughter of a Scottish earl, living in Glamis Castle in the Highlands."

"Trust you to admire the Scottish royal," muttered Geoffrey.

Elizabeth ignored him. "She was very charming and not just a social butterfly, either! During the First World War, her family used their castle as a convalescent home for soldiers. And Elizabeth worked as a nurse, even though she was only fifteen at the time."

"She does not sound like you in the least," Geoffrey remarked.

"Anyway, she got to know the King's younger son, Bertie, and when he asked her to marry him, she turned him down."

"She seems to have had a clearer view of royal life than you do, dear."

Elizabeth ignored him. "He kept proposing to her, though, and—get this! His parents—the King and Queen, mind you!—said to him, 'You'll be a lucky fellow if *she* accepts you.' Imagine being *that* approved of."

"And were they right?"

"They were. She was marvelous. They got married in 1923, and when she entered Westminster Abbey for the wedding, she laid her bouquet on the grave of the unknown warrior and walked to the altar without it. And during World War II, she actually practiced with a pistol at Windsor, because, she said, if the Nazis invaded England, she wanted to go down fighting. I would like very much to meet *her*."

"And her wedding song was . . . ?"

"'Lead Us Heavenly Father.'"

"I think you ought to go for that one," said Geoffrey. "It will have sentimental associations for you. Assuming, of course, that you can find anyone around here who can sing it."

"Yes, I hope I have better luck with musicians than I did with caterers. Did you hear about Charles's recommendation?"

"Yes," murmured Geoffrey, looking troubled. "Charles is behaving oddly these days. And don't say 'How perfectly normal,' because I know that he's always peculiar, but he's being strange in a different way."

"Do you think he's up to something?"

Geoffrey hesitated. "I think he bears watching."

◆ ◆ ◆

THE SHERIFF'S READING glasses were perched on the end of his nose as he examined the blue cloisonné urn on his desk. Cautiously he picked it up and checked to make sure that the lid was on tight before examining the bottom. "Made in China," he announced with a sigh of disgust. "That's no help."

"Yeah, I noticed that. It's heavy, though, isn't it?" asked Clay, who had just finished photographing the urn and dusting it for prints.

"There's something in there, all right. I was hoping

for a serial number, or—if we were really lucky—the name of a funeral home inscribed on the bottom."

The deputy shook his head. "It's never that easy."

"It is in real life." Wesley grinned. "Remember the fool who tried to hold up the bank in Decatur, and wrote his holdup note on his own deposit slip?"

"Well, in this case you're out of luck. You've got no clues as to the origin of the vase; no fingerprints, thanks to five years of Clarine's diligent housekeeping; and no trace of the packaging that the vase was sent in, also thanks to the widow's cleaning mania." He took a long swallow of coffee and made a face. Wesley Rountree could not make coffee worth a damn. "I think you're going to have to open it."

"You're right," sighed Wesley. "I reckon it could just be filled with sand. Before we go any farther in looking into this matter, we have to know."

He wiped his hands against his trouser legs and took a flat-footed stance facing the desk. Cradling the urn in the crook of his arm, Wesley gripped the lid and turned. After a moment's hesitation, it turned easily, and within seconds he had set it back on the desktop and lifted the lid.

"It isn't sand," he said, peering at the contents of the urn. "It isn't fine ash, either."

The deputy ambled over to Wesley's desk to take a look. "There's chunks of stuff in there," he said. "What is that? Bone?"

"Looks like it," the sheriff agreed. "So we have *some-body* in this urn, even if it isn't Emmet Mason."

"Yeah, but who?"

"Let me think about this," said Wesley, running a hand across his bristly hair. "I need to talk it out and see what occurs to me. Five years ago Emmet leaves for California on a business trip. . . ."

"Did he?"

"Good question. We know he's dead there now, but we don't know that he went there then. What we do know is that five years ago Clarine Mason got a phone call, purporting to come from California, telling her that her husband was dead."

"But you can make a phone call from anywhere," Clay pointed out.

"True. And then she got a package, containing this blue urn, supposedly filled with the ashes of her cremated husband."

"But since we don't have the wrapping and since she never looked at it, we don't know that the package actually came from California." The deputy shook his head. "I don't think that narrows it down a whole lot, Wesley."

The sheriff leaned back in his swivel chair and closed his eyes. "I am trying to remember Emmet Mason," he said. "Friendly fellow, kind of beefy. Ran the hardware store, but wasn't too interested in tools himself, as far as I could tell. He was big in little theatre, though. He'd lived here all his life. The Masons have been here for a good hundred years. They built that homestead where Clarine lives now before the Civil War."

"So?"

"I've got to call Clarine. Why don't you get on the other line and call around to all the funeral homes in the area."

"What for?"

"Ask if any of them do cremations."

◆　◆　◆

CHARLES CHANDLER figured that it was a long shot, at best, considering the amount of time he had at his disposal—ten days, at the most—but he felt that he owed it to himself and his potential as a scientist to make an effort.

With that in mind, he had dressed in his most conventional outfit: khaki slacks, a navy blue blazer, and an ugly yellow tie borrowed from Geoffrey, who evidently prized it. Now, clean-shaven and smelling like Old Spice, he was ready to make a Serious Effort in the matrimonial sweepstakes. He needed the million dollars.

The problem was that he had no idea how to go about locating a suitable young woman. Like Geoffrey, Charles had gone to prep school away from

Chandler Grove. After that had come college and the colony of scientists, as Charles liked to call them. He hardly knew anyone in Chandler Grove anymore, a fact that until recently was a source of comfort to him, since he found idle socializing both frightening and time-consuming.

The sudden need of a marriage partner had shed rather a different light on his freedom from social obligation. Now he felt like an outcast, marooned in a strange land whose language he did not speak. Even the most casual encounter made him feel like an alien. What *did* one reply to the man in a camouflage hunting outfit and a University of Georgia cap who ambled up to him at the gas station and said, "How 'bout them Dawgs?" Charles said that he didn't own one, which, judging from the man's reaction, was not the correct response.

Charles was afraid that he might find the female residents of Chandler Grove equally impossible to communicate with. He tried to think of places that he could locate someone who was more of a kindred spirit. He had still received no reply to the letter he had sent to the *Georgian Highlander* box number. Surely the responses to such a local magazine couldn't be *that* numerous; perhaps his literary skills were even worse than he feared. Should he try again? There were Atlanta newspapers and magazines with personals columns for lonely yuppies, but they also required a writ-

ten reply to a post office box, and there wasn't time
for that. He needed somebody around here that he
could relate to. Some other group of outsiders, perhaps, who were in Chandler Grove but not *of* it.

Earthling!

Charles remembered the group of Earth Shoe people described by Tommy Simmons. Charles had recommended them as caterers for Elizabeth's wedding
partly out of mischief and partly because as a vegetarian himself, he hoped that his cousin would hire
them to cater the wedding so that he could enjoy the
food. Now he thought of an even better use for Earthling: as a source of suitable women.

Having forgotten exactly where the lawyer had said
they were, Charles had to drive about in search of
their health-food store. Fortunately, in Chandler
Grove, such a quest was not difficult. After ten minutes of driving, he crossed the steel span bridge over
the river, having covered the one-block business district of downtown Chandler Grove without finding
any new establishments. Once over the river he discovered what he was looking for. The old gristmill,
set in a grove of ancient oaks, had been repainted barn
red and displayed a sign over its porch—EARTHLING—
with a logo: a rainbow over an oak tree.

He parked the family station wagon in the gravel
lot next to the riverbank and went in, hoping that a
maiden with the soul of Madame Curie and the looks

of Joan Baez was waiting for her prince to come. He straightened his borrowed tie.

Perhaps he had overdressed for the part, he thought, looking over the Earthling premises. A sawdust-covered floor was littered with packing crates and barrels of grain, each labeled with a sign hand-lettered in Magic Marker. A homemade cloth banner on one wall proclaimed the back room as the national headquarters for the Central American Prayer and Protest Group. Charles edged his way past plastic tubs of spices to examine the notices on the bulletin board. He had worked his way through *Goat's Milk for Sale*; *Custom-made Crystal Jewelry*; and *Advanced Yoga Classes* when a gaunt, bearded man emerged from the back room and hailed him with "Yo! How can I help?"

Charles took a deep breath. "I—uh—" Inspiration! "I notice you have a sign up about Central America and I wondered if I could help."

The man stared at Charles in his suit jacket and tie. "Well, we have a beans-and-rice dinner coming up on Friday night."

"No. That wasn't what I had in mind. Look, are you part of the underground?"

"I beg your pardon?"

"You know, the *underground*! That group that smuggles political refugees out of Costa Rica!"

A woman with braids and rimless glasses stuck her

head out from behind the curtained doorway. "There aren't any refugees from Costa Rica."

"Puerto Rico, then," said Charles impatiently. He wished he had taken a look at *Newsweek* before he left home. "You know, Central American illegal aliens."

The Earthlings looked at each other and shrugged. This guy was too dumb to work for immigration, they figured, and it didn't seem worth the trouble to enlighten him in regard to Puerto Rico.

"I thought I might marry one," Charles said wildly. "Keep her from being deported."

The woman's lips twitched in amusement, but she said nothing.

Finally the man said gently, "We don't do aliens. Look, can I help you?"

Charles looked at them, trying to decide whether or not to tell the truth. Better not, he decided. They didn't appear to be people who would do desperate things for a large sum of money. They would for a cause, of course, but he couldn't come up with one on short notice.

The woman came out from behind the curtain now, looking concerned. Her lips were pale and her eyelids red with a well-scrubbed look. Charles thought that she looked sympathetic and her figure was all right.

"Look," he said, "I'm a physicist, and I don't know anybody in town. Would you go out to dinner with me and tell me all about your work here?"

The woman regarded him as if he were a weevil in the whole-wheat flour. "No way," she said.

◆   ◆   ◆

WHILE HE WAITED FOR his deputy to get off the phone, Wesley stared up at the picture of the cowgirl on the palomino. The girl and the horse graced the calendar above his desk. Every year Wesley would sift through the collection of complimentary calendars sent out by local businesses—in search of a new palomino and cowgirl to adorn his workspace. Usually it was the feed store or the local hardware that issued such an offering, but this year they had opted for collie puppies and waterfalls, respectively, so Wesley had had to go as far as the Milton's Forge Tack and Saddle Store. This year's cowgirl, a skinny blonde in a white buckskin jacket, looked as if the palomino she was holding by the reins was the first of its species she had encountered. Wesley would be glad when the year was over. There weren't any trees in the background, either. Any place without trees made him nervous.

His conversation with Clarine Mason had been brief. He had told her as gently as possible that the photograph from California did resemble Emmet, as far as he could tell, and that being the case, he had a few more questions to ask. He wanted to know if Emmet had ever been to college or if he had lived anywhere but Chandler Grove. Clarine said that apparently he had, if he was presently residing on a slab in a Los Angeles morgue, but Wesley assured her that he meant *before* that, to the best of her knowledge.

"No," said Clarine Mason, without a moment's hesitation. "He went to the community college for a business course, but he'd lived at home then. Of course, there's the army. He was stationed in Germany about 1960. Does that count?"

"It may count," said Wesley, "But I doubt if it matters." He told her that he would be in touch when he learned anything and hung up.

Clay, on the other hand, seemed to get trapped by every person he talked to. He always wound up saying very little during these phone conversations, except for an occasional "I understand" and "That's not really why I called" or "How interesting." The calls always started out the same way. Clay would inquire whether the funeral homes supervised cremations, and then he wouldn't get a word in edgewise for a good three minutes. Wesley was afraid that if this kept up, his deputy would become a real-estate baron in cemetery plots.

Finally, on the last call, he managed to avoid having one of the firm's representatives sent around to discuss their special prepayment burial plan (*Because in your line of work, sir, you never know*) and he hung up the phone with the air of one who has had to wrest himself from its clutches.

"Okay," he said, turning to Wesley. "I have some information for you. And, listen, if anybody with a voice like Vincent Price calls up and asks for me, tell 'em I'm out, all right?"

"Persistent, were they?" Wesley chuckled. "What did you find out?"

"They didn't want to discuss cremation, you understand. I gather it must not be a profitable enterprise for them. It does them out of embalming charges, expensive vaults, satin-lined caskets, and all that other good stuff that contributes to the high cost of dying." Clay shook his head. "When I go, just wrap me in a blanket and throw me in the ground."

"That's probably illegal," Wesley pointed out.

"Yeah, they got lobbyists in the legislature, too, don't they?" He turned to the page of scribbled notes he had taken during the phone calls. "All right, most of the local ones say that they don't offer the service because there's no demand for cremations in rural areas. Especially not back East. Now, in places like California, Hawaii, and Oregon, about forty percent of the deceased are cremated, but in, say, Kentucky and Tennessee, the figure is less than one percent."

"Land is cheaper here," Wesley remarked. "Also, we're conservative here in the Bible Belt. In Sunday school they taught us that resurrection of the body would take place on Judgment Day, and by God it's hard to agree to have your remains incinerated if there's even a tiny chance you'd be missing out on a chance to come back."

"Oh, Wesley, that makes no sense. Why, decomposition of human remains—"

"I didn't say it made sense," the sheriff retorted. "But I'll bet you it accounts for the ninety-nine percent who want an old-fashioned burial."

"It's not environmentally sound," said Clay with the conviction of the newly converted. "One guy—Clarence Calloway, over at Shady Pines in Reedsville—allows as how cremation is a pretty good idea, even though they don't offer it. He says that in the United States, a person dies every fifteen seconds, making a grand total of fifty-seven hundred bodies a day to be disposed of. That's a lot of land going into cemetery plots. And every new cemetery means less forest, less farmland, and less living space for those that *are* living."

"That's a pretty convincing argument," Wesley conceded. "So how come he's not offering this service if it's such a good idea?"

"He can't afford to," said Clay. "First of all, like I said, there's not so much profit margin in cremation as there is in regular burial, and secondly, in order to do it, you have to have a lot of expensive equipment. Now if there's such a small demand for cremation in this area, you'd never recoup your investment."

"Well, suppose Mr. Calloway's funeral home does get that rare ecological patriot who doesn't want to take up space in the ground. What do they do about him?"

"They farm it out," said Clay, consulting his notes again. "I have it written down here. It seems that there is one place in this area that has a crematorium, and what few families request it are sent over there."

Wesley picked up his pen. "Now we're getting somewhere. Who is it?"

"It's called Elijah's Chariot, Inc., and it's over in Roan County." Clay shook his head in bewilderment over the name. "You reckon they named the business that because of the association? Chariot of fire, I mean. Kind of a poetic term for cremation."

"Could be," said Wesley, "but if I remember my Sunday-school classes right, it means something a whole lot more interesting."

"Want to go over and talk to them tomorrow?"

"I have to be in court tomorrow, but if I get out in time, I will. Before then, though, I want to know who's in that urn."

"Who's going to tell you that?"

Wesley grinned. "An expert witness."

◆　◆　◆

CLARINE MASON WAS on her second straight glass of Southern Comfort. No ice, for once; she wanted it neat. In case anyone should drop by she had put a dish of mints beside her chair. She wouldn't want her neighbors to smell liquor on her breath. Clarine had fixed her hair in a French twist, and she'd put on her navy blue church dress—just in case. She had asked the sheriff not to tell anyone the news about Emmet, and he'd said he wouldn't, but she got dressed up anyway. It occurred to her that she might like to talk about this strange new feeling of bereavement, but it was too embarrassing to be shared.

The first grief had been a clean wound. Five years ago, she had felt anger at Emmet for his foolishness—and the pain at losing him and her security and her identity as Mrs. Somebody, so important in a small community. But she had everyone's sympathy, and no one could say it was her fault back then. She had *told* Emmet not to go.

This time, though, there was a comic element to her dilemma that undermined her dignity as a widow. People would naturally be wondering what Emmet had been up to for five years. And now, instead of being a tragic widow, Clarine would be regarded as just another discarded middle-aged woman whose husband had gone off to greener pastures.

She stared up at the empty spot on the mantelpiece where Emmet's picture had resided. It was strange that she should feel a new surge of grief, when in her mind Emmet had already been dead for five years. It was as if the phone call from California had brought her husband back to life for a few moments, only to let him die all over again.

And if she had been able to speak to him between one death and the other, what would she have said? That she missed him? That she wanted him back? Or would she have spent it in recriminations for his cruelty and his cowardice? Clarine took another swig of her drink, knowing the answer and not liking it.

She wondered if she would be expected to go to California now to clean up whatever mess Emmet had left in his five extra years of existence. Was there a young wife out there left with bills to pay? A new insurance policy to be contested? New possessions to be disposed of? Clarine decided that she didn't care. The Emmet Mason whose wife she had been had died five years ago. What came after that would have to be someone else's problem.

◆ ◆ ◆

IN A SLIDING METAL tray in a Los Angeles morgue, the body of a man in late middle age lay in peaceful repose. The end had not been peaceful, and there had been a good deal of pain reflected in his heavy-featured face during the first moments of death, but that had been smoothed away now, and within the cold confines of the metal drawer, the body was flaccid and younger looking than it had been in some years.

There was some irony in this, because during the last years of his life the man had gone to some trouble to attain a more youthful appearance. He had exercised regularly in a somewhat ungainly manner, in baggy sweatpants that elicited smiles from his fellow joggers. He had tanned his body and dieted on wheat germ and yogurt—in an attempt to banish cholesterol and flab from his well-padded frame.

His efforts had not achieved the desired effect. He looked not younger, as he had imagined, but rather pathetic, like a man trying desperately to be what he wasn't: young, good-looking, virile. No one at any distance, no matter how dim the light, had ever mistaken him for any of those things, during those last five years.

He did not look successful, because he wasn't. He was a down-at-heels salesclerk who went to auditions on his days off and he lived in a shabby single room that cost more than he would have thought possible. The new life didn't come to much. In the end, the only youth restorative for a man his age is the tonic of wealth and power. Lacking those qualities, he was invisible to the golden young women who jogged past him on the beach. He was as sexless as their fathers. He was faintly ridiculous.

It was this fear of a ridicule already felt that kept him where he was. Each time he lifted a telephone and got as far as the 404 area code of Georgia, a dread of the derision that would await him back home froze him into retreat. He never made the call to see if he could be forgiven, to ask to go home. Really, though, he didn't want to go home. He only wanted them to respect him from a distance, after he had achieved his long-sought success.

He could only hope that someday one of the auditions would pay off and that an acting part—no matter how small—would establish his worth and the rightness of his decision. But it never happened. Instead, on one such quest of a ticket to Equity, he daydreamed too long on a boring stretch of freeway and found himself in the wrong lane for his exit. To pass it by would be unthinkable; it would cost him half an hour and make him late for the audition. So he swerved, trying to force his way into the relentless stream of traffic, but the engine on his Concord—an automotive version of himself—was not equal to the maneuver, and he found himself broadsided by a new and shiny Mercedes. His last thought as he crashed through the guardrail was that Sam Peckinpah had been right: you really *did* die in slow motion.

CHAPTER

9

IT WAS PELTING DOWN rain. In the foyer of Old
St. Andrews House Adam McIver looked out at the
gray sky and hunched his Burberry tighter around him
in preparation for the dash outside. He thought the
sudden downpour might be his punishment for leaving work a bit early today, but he had a dinner party
to go to that evening and he needed the extra time.

"Hello!" said a soft voice from behind him. "Not afraid of getting wet, are you?"

Adam turned around to see the Princess of Wales smiling up at him. He gave her a friendly nod, as he was quite used to seeing her by now. He encountered Princess Dianas nearly every day, shopping for vegetables in the market, queuing up for buses, and waiting tables at the Roxburghe Hotel. Even one of his sister's flatmates had adopted the look; of course, you had to take into account the fact that the flatmate was an air hostess. Still, it seemed to Adam that every young blonde in the kingdom had adopted that bob-and-fringe hairstyle and the ruffled blouse and Fair Isle wardrobe. This one was a better likeness than most: she had a good straight nose and sensible eye makeup. Adam hated the ones who looked like raccoons.

"I'm not a bit afraid of the rain," he protested, trying to place her. "But I was a fool to forget my wellies."

"Well, it is June," she replied, in a distinct Morningside accent. "You ought to be able to count on good weather some of the time."

"Oh, you can. Whenever you happen to be in Spain," Adam replied. He remembered her now. She was the administrative assistant that he had spoken to about getting Dawson's American fiancée invited to the garden party. "How are arrangements going for the Royal Garden Party?" he asked, to prove that he recognized her.

She made a moue of distaste at being asked to talk shop. "Just as usual. Not many changes, you know, from one year to the next, except perhaps Her Majesty's outfit, and oddly enough, no one can ever remember what she wore."

"All the arrangements under way by now, are they?"

"I rang up Black and Edgington in Greenock today. Of course, they always provide the props, you know: chairs, tablecloths, marquees, so they hardly need to be reminded. I'm sure they know the drill better than I do."

"And will you be making the biscuits?" asked Adam, attempting to be witty.

The response was a wide-eyed stare. "Certainly not! Crawford's Catering of Leith always does that. There'll be cream cakes, scones, and small sandwiches. It's the same every year. The guest list is rather predictable, too. The usual company directors and civil-service types, of course. Scottish Sloanes always go, and those who just missed getting on the honours list are asked as a consolation prize."

Adam nodded. "I'm Adam McIver," he told her. "I helped compose the list."

"Well, it was all right," the blonde said kindly. "Quite an average list, in fact. At least, I didn't notice any blunders. I thought it was much the same as last year. I didn't notice your name on it, though."

The young bureaucrat reddened. "Well, I hardly thought—that is, nobody told me—"

"Would you like to go? I'm sure I can arrange it. It's a dreadful bun fight, but you can always go out for tea later, can't you? The Queen makes most people too nervous to eat anyhow."

"I would love to go," said Adam. "It's very kind of you to offer."

"No bother. What's one more face in that great crush? Eight thousand, you know. For tea. It's a bit late for you to be asked, but I expect I can manage. Especially seeing as you're one of our lot." A civil servant, she meant.

"I'm afraid I've already made a bit of trouble for you, though. You've already had to scrounge that invitation for the Dawsons. He's an old acquaintance of mine who's getting married this month, and he wanted to bring the new wife. Did you manage to sort that out?"

She looked stern. "Yes, of course we did. Her Majesty's guests must be treated with the utmost courtesy. Reasonable requests from them are granted whenever possible." Her voice dropped to a whisper. "I can tell you, though, my boss was quite narky about it."

"I was afraid he would be." Adam sighed. "But I

hadn't any choice. The guest is an old school friend of mine, and his American bride seems quite set on it. You know how the Yanks are about the royals."

Princess Diana nodded. "I do indeed!"

◆   ◆   ◆

AUNT AMANDA'S upstairs sitting room had been turned into command headquarters for the duration of the wedding preparations. Notes, price lists, and phone numbers were tacked to a message board propped up on the mantelpiece, and in the center of the chaos of bridal items, Aunt Amanda herself directed operations with the brisk efficiency of a field marshal.

The bride-to-be, looking most unromantic in faded jeans and an Edinburgh T-shirt, was sitting on the chintz sofa with her legs tucked up behind her, leafing through a back issue of *Bride's*.

"Let's just make sure that we have everything straight now," said Aunt Amanda, peering at Elizabeth over the top of her reading glasses.

Elizabeth put down the magazine and searched through the papers on the coffee table for her own copy of the list marked *Wedding—To Do*. "All right. I found it."

"The invitations are addressed and mailed?"

"Check. Some time ago."

"The minister has been asked." Amanda put a star beside that item on her list. "I did that by telephone. He said that he would drop by to meet the two of you when Cameron arrives. When is that, by the way?"

"The middle of next week. They're flying in to Atlanta. Uncle Robert is picking them up."

"Good. I was afraid you'd want to go along, but it's out of the question. We have very little time as it is. Let's see. What's next. Ah! The caterers have been notified?"

Elizabeth hesitated. "I spoke to Earthling, but is there anyone else we could get to do the reception?"

"Whatever is the matter? Can't they manage a simple wedding reception?" Aunt Amanda looked stern. "You didn't ask for haggis, did you?"

Elizabeth explained about Rogan Josh and his politically inspired menu. "I just didn't think I could cope with him. If I argued with him, I'd feel like a social oppressor and if I didn't, I'd feel that I'd been bullied by a crank. I don't know what to do."

Amanda Chandler's expression changed from bewilderment to annoyance. "Leave them to me!" Her eyes flashed.

"Gladly. I went to the florist yesterday—the one you recommended."

"Oh, yes. Lucy in Chandler Grove. I've always been pleased with her work. She did the—" Amanda's voice faltered. "You know, the funerals."

Elizabeth reddened, babbling on to cover the awkwardness. "We had quite a nice talk. I ended up telling her all about forensic anthropology, and she told me that a florist leads a more interesting life than you'd think. Apparently, the sheriff had consulted her about something that day."

"You haven't time to stand about gossiping with shopkeepers. Did you happen to choose the flowers?"

"Oh, she was very helpful. I think I have all the planning taken care of for the decorations. She's doing baskets of spring flowers for the house—I told her I didn't care what was in those. I expect she knows best about arrangements. And for the bouquet we compromised."

"How so?"

"I wanted white roses and white heather, but she says heather is out of the question. She thinks she can get thistles, though. They grow wild in the mountains at this time of year."

"Be careful how you carry it then," Amanda advised. "Thistles and roses. That's a lot of thorns. Aren't you worried about the symbolism?"

"The thistle is the symbol of Scotland, so I thought I was all right on that score. Besides, you can go crazy if you worry too much about symbolism."

"Which brings us to *something old, something new. . . .*"

"I'll worry about that later!"

"But do you have a sixpence? That's the last line you know: *And a sixpence in her shoe.*"

"I'll call Cameron. They don't use them anymore, of course, since Britain went off the lovely monetary system they used to have for a boring old decimal system. I expect he can find one, though. What's next?"

"Flowers for the bridesmaid, boutonniere for the groom and ushers, corsages for the mothers."

"All done. Cameron is getting one white rosebud and a thistle for his boutonniere."

"And your attendants?"

"Red roses, white baby's breath, and thistles, with tartan ribbon."

Amanda nodded her approval. "That brings us to the wedding gown. I cannot believe that you have left it this late."

Elizabeth sucked in her stomach. "I was waiting until the last possible pound," she admitted.

"Well, have you any idea what you want?"

Elizabeth nodded. "I thought I'd buy a pattern and material and have it made. You do have a seamstress around here, don't you? Because otherwise: malls of Atlanta, here I come."

"We have a seamstress, *if* she is not already too busy. This is bride season, you know. Fortunately prom time is past. Her name is Miss Geneva Grey. She and her sister Aurelia used to do quite a bit of fine sewing. Their father was a country doctor here years ago, even before your Uncle Robert went into practice. Old Dr. Grey was one of the founders of the county hospital. His daughters never married. They kept that big old house all by themselves and they do sewing as much to keep busy as for the money. Though I suppose in these days of taxation, everyone could use more money."

"Probably so," said Elizabeth, whose thoughts were elsewhere.

"The sisters were very different, though. Geneva was the shy one, but Aurelia had spunk. We were all quite surprised that she should be the first to go. Passed away on a trip to Florida."

Elizabeth was more concerned with her wedding gown than with local gossip. "But the surviving sister still does sewing?" she persisted.

"Of course. Miss Geneva tries to accommodate everyone who needs sewing done."

"I'll call her right now," Elizabeth promised. "I'll need to get Jenny in for a fitting, too."

Before they arrived at the next order of business, the door chimes sounded. "I'll get it," said Elizabeth. "It's probably the UPS truck bringing more wedding presents."

Aunt Amanda drew aside the curtain and peered down at the driveway. "I don't think so. There's a sheriff's car parked on the circle."

"I'll go anyway," said Elizabeth. "I wonder what he wants."

◆　◆　◆

IN EDINBURGH IT was seven P.M., still broad daylight in this land near the midnight sun, but time for dinner, anyhow. Cameron Dawson and his mother and younger brother were sitting in the small dining room, eating the first course of their meal: homemade cucumber soup. Traveller the cat, while too proud to beg, was lying under the sideboard in readiness, just in case anything should fall from the table.

"No mail today, then?" asked Cameron, tilting his bowl away from him to get the last bit of soup.

"No," said Margaret Dawson. "Only some bits of advertising."

"What were you expecting?" asked Ian. "Wedding presents?"

"Actually, I thought we might be due for another postcard," his brother replied. "That gnome is certainly getting around, isn't he?"

They glanced out the window at the sunny garden, where a bare patch of earth under a bush was the only trace of the missing garden ornament.

Ian nodded. "He's been to Alaska, Italy, and Ibiza. There seems to be no pattern to it. I wonder where he'll turn up next. Hong Kong, perhaps? He seems about due for Asia."

"Melbourne," Cameron suggested.

"Have you any idea who is doing this?" asked Margaret. "It seems to me a very odd sort of joke."

Ian shook his head. "I have asked every lunatic I know," he said. "Honestly. I even rang up the ones in Aberdeen and Glasgow. They all swear they didn't do it—but they wish they'd thought of it!"

"Now you've done it!" his mother remarked cheerfully. "There'll be a rash of gnome thefts in Scotland! Anyhow, that's one set of friends accounted for. What about yours, Cameron?"

"*Mine?*" cried young Dr. Dawson, with an expression of wounded dignity. "None of my friends would stoop to such a thing. You might as well ask the minister if *he* did it!"

"Cameron has a point," said Ian, reaching for the bread. "None of his friends has the nerve to pull it off, much less the imagination. You don't suppose it was the minister?" he added hopefully.

His mother shook her head. "None of my friends finds it funny. They all think it's a prelude to a burglary. I must say they have me quite worried about leaving home."

"Nonsense!" said Cameron. "We've enlisted the entire neighborhood to watch the house. It will be perfectly all right to go."

"It's a pity we can't contact the gnome and tell him that we'll be leaving home shortly," Margaret Dawson mused. "Suppose he writes us while we're off in America."

"Then Dr. Grant will keep the card for us until we get back, just as he's doing with the rest of the mail," said Ian reasonably. "Honestly, you act as if it's a lost dog we're talking about."

"Well, it does seem quite alive now that it's corresponding with us, doesn't it?" She looked thoughtful. "Although it never says anything *personal*, does it? It never addresses us by name on the cards, or says anything about seals or estate agents, or anything that would indicate that he knows much about us."

"It's hard to eavesdrop when you're stuck out under a forsythia bush in the garden," Ian pointed out.

"No, I see what she means," said Cameron. "We can't tell from the postcards whether the people who took the gnome are personally acquainted with us or not."

"I think they must be," said Margaret Dawson. "But I can't imagine who it is."

"A salesman, perhaps?" suggested Ian. "Someone who travels frequently on business? Maybe someone in the North Sea oil industry? An RAF pilot? Do any of us know someone like that?"

They all shook their heads. No one of their acquaintance fit such a description.

"Well," said Margaret Dawson, collecting the empty soup bowls, "we're off to America next week. I wonder where our garden gnome will be going next?"

◆ ◆ ◆

WHEN ELIZABETH OPENED the front door, she found Sheriff Wesley Rountree standing on the porch, wearing his khaki uniform and dress Stetson. He was holding a large blue cloisonné vase.

"Come in!" cried Elizabeth, ushering him into the hall. "It is so nice to see you again, Sheriff. I haven't seen you since . . ." She faltered. The mention of one cousin's murder and another cousin's guilt would be inappropriate on a social occasion, she thought. "Well, I had no idea you'd remember me after all this time," she went on happily. "But this is so *nice* of you. You really shouldn't have!"

"Uh . . . well, ma'am . . . I mean . . ."

The sheriff seemed at a loss for words, but Elizabeth, who wasn't, took no notice of his reply. "This is such a lovely vase!" she cried. "I'll just put it on the table with the rest of the wedding gifts. Really, this is so sweet of you, Sheriff. You shouldn't have!"

Wesley cleared his throat loudly. "The fact is, ma'am, I didn't!" he called to her as she hurried away with the vase.

Elizabeth turned in midstride, her smile still plastered in place. "Beg your pardon?"

"About that vase," said Wesley, who had just remembered to take his hat off. "I apologize for the misunderstanding and I just feel like a hill of beans about it. But what with you being a bride and all, I can certainly understand how you'd come to the conclusion you did." Wesley had a theory that apologies sounded more sincere in Southern dialect and he always adjusted his accent accordingly.

Elizabeth looked down at the blue vase and then back at the sheriff, still confused about the purpose of the visit.

"It isn't a wedding present at all," Wesley explained. "And I'm sure you won't want it when I tell you what it *is*."

Elizabeth contemplated the blue enamel jar, which—she now noticed—had a lid and felt too heavy to be empty. "Oh shit," she whispered, setting the object on the coffee table.

Wesley looked at her sadly. "I see you figured it out, ma'am."

"Call me Elizabeth," she said. "Now sit down here and tell me what you're doing wandering around Chandler Grove with a funeral urn."

Wesley settled in on the sofa and explained about Emmet Mason's encore performance as a traffic fatality, which had naturally led to curiosity on the part of his widow as to just *who* had been sitting in the middle of her mantelpiece in a blue metal urn for the last five years. "And when I read the announcement about your engagement in the local paper—for which congratulations, by the way—I couldn't help noticing that you were a forensic anthropologist. So I said to myself, *Now there's the person I need to talk to about this!*" Wesley beamed at the clarity of his explanation.

Elizabeth blinked. "You want to consult me on a case?"

"I do. You are the one who's studying forensic anthropology, aren't you?"

"Yes."

"And you've had some experience analyzing human remains and so on?"

"A couple of years, yes."

"Then I sure would appreciate it if you could give me some expert opinions here."

Elizabeth raised her eyebrows. "Surely the state of Georgia has people who do this."

"Whole crowds of them, I expect," said Wesley amiably. "But they don't hang out around these parts. So if I wanted to consult one of them, I'd have to take a day off from regular duties, which would play hell with the patrol schedules, and the county would probably have to pay them a consulting fee, which I expect I would hear about from the board of commissioners."

Elizabeth nodded. "Go on."

"Now I wouldn't mind the consulting fee if there was a crime involved, but I can't be sure of that. Why, for all I know that could be pig's knuckles stuck in that jar. Besides that, going off to hunt up a consultant in Atlanta would take up time, and out of consideration for that poor Mrs. Mason—she's the widow—I wanted to get some answers to this just as quick as I could. She's mighty upset, as I'm sure you can understand. So I thought that the fastest and easiest recourse would be to drive over here and ask you two questions."

"What two questions?"

Wesley's face took on a solemn expression, which meant that having charmed his way into a free consultation with a medical expert, he was ready to talk business—and to learn something. "Can you tell anything from cremated remains?"

"Yes."

"What can you tell?"

Elizabeth's lips twitched in the briefest of smiles. "Is that your second question?"

"No. Rephrasing of the first. Could you elaborate on that first answer, please?"

"Okay. Most people think that the ashes of a cremated person will look like the residue you find in a wood-burning fireplace: fine, papery ash. But that is not the case. Human remains *can* be made to look that way, if they are milled after the cremation process is complete, but unless the family requests that, it usually isn't done. The general rule is: if you tell the mortuary that the ashes are going to be scattered, they will be more likely to mill them, but if you plan to just keep the ashes in an urn in a vault, or"—she shrugged—"on a mantelpiece, then they'll just put them in the container the way they look when they come out of the furnace."

Wesley grimaced. "Not a pleasant topic of conversation, is it?"

"Not one I expected to be having this week," admitted the bride-to-be.

"Well, I understand all that you've said so far," said Wesley. "You go right on explaining."

"If the remains in this urn have been milled, there may not be much I can learn from them. I'd advise you to start hunting up experts with high-tech labs in that case, and maybe even *they*—"

"They didn't look milled to me," Wesley remarked. Blushing a little, he added, "I've looked."

"Okay, well, let me see what we've got. Could you hand me a newspaper from that basket by the fireplace?"

The sheriff looked startled. "Don't you want to take this to the hospital or something?"

"No. What for?" Elizabeth smiled. "The evidence isn't microscopic, Sheriff. I'll be able to tell you everything I can after a couple of minutes' examination.

And all I have to do is look at it. Of course, there *are* other tests: cross-sectioning a tooth or—"

"I'll settle for the general opinion just now," said Wesley, anticipating another lecture.

"Okay. Let's just dump it out here on the coffee table. Spread out the newspaper, please."

Wesley laid out several thicknesses of the *Atlanta Constitution* on the Chandlers' marble-topped coffee table. Elizabeth pried the lid loose from the jar and gently sprinkled the contents into a pile in the center of the table.

"Yes," she said, fingering the mound of charred matter. "This is what unmilled cremated remains looks like. Some ash interspersed with objects that don't burn at that temperature—bits of bone, tooth, metal tooth fillings, and so on."

"Are you ready for the second question?" asked Wesley, watching her sort the fragments with a practiced touch.

"Sure. Go ahead."

"Is this a calf or something?"

Elizabeth looked at him. "You kind of wish it were, don't you?" she said softly. "You're afraid somebody got murdered to give Mr. Mason a body to stuff in the urn."

"That had occurred to me," Wesley admitted.

"You can get a second opinion on all this, of course. Get somebody who already has a Ph.D. and an official lab to confirm what I tell you. You just want to know if it's worth it to send it off to be analyzed, right?"

The sheriff nodded. "That was my intention. If you told me it was the contents of a pipe smoker's ashtray, I wouldn't bother, but if there's something potentially criminal here, why, I can justify the expense of having it analyzed. Are you saying you can't tell what I've got here?"

"Oh, I can," said Elizabeth. "But I'd rather not have the responsibility." She smiled up at him. "In case you have to go to court with this while I'm on my honeymoon."

Wesley raised his right hand. "On my honor I won't call you to testify as an expert witness. Now tell me what that stuff is."

"I'm afraid that it is human remains," said Elizabeth softly.

Wesley nodded. "I had a hunch it would be."

She held up a small bonelike bit. "You see that? It's a human cuspid. Front tooth. And this little bit here is the metal from a filling. Probably a molar." She rummaged around the sooty pile for a few moments longer. "This is a bit of vertebra and this splintered bit is part of a long bone. See? There's quite a bit left."

"I thought of a third question," said Wesley.

"I expect you have," murmured Elizabeth, still examining the contents of the urn. "You want to know if I can give you any particulars about who's in here, don't you?"

"Is that possible?"

No answer was forthcoming. The sheriff noticed that the young woman beside him had suddenly tensed up, and her expression had shifted from casual interest to one of alertness. "That's funny," she muttered to herself.

Wesley peered at the scraps of bone, but he could see nothing to have quickened her interest. There was no flattened bullet in the ashes; nothing spectacular as far as *he* could see. Elizabeth seemed to be sifting out tiny brackets of metal, of two different sizes, and collecting them in a pile at the edge of the newspaper.

"What did you find?" he asked.

Elizabeth shook her head. "More than you bargained for, Sheriff."

◆　◆　◆

CHARLES CHANDLER WAS getting desperate. The wedding was just over a week away, and he wasn't even engaged. He hadn't even met anybody. The prospects of inheriting his aunt Augusta's wealth seemed dimmer all the time. Snow White from the *Highlander Magazine* had not responded to his letter and he was running out of ideas. Where did one meet marriage-minded women? Where would one find a woman who liked physics?

His own prep-school physics teacher had been a bearded gentleman named Fallowfield; otherwise, Charles might have come up with the idea sooner. As it was, he was actually driving past the grounds of the county high school before it occurred to him that science teachers would understand his work. They might even *like* him. And a multimillion-dollar estate would make a nice change from living on a teacher's salary.

On impulse, he turned into the school driveway and pulled into the gravel parking lot for faculty. There was no difficulty in finding a parking place; since it was nearly July, the students were no longer attending school, but the number of cars in the lot indicated that the teachers were still on the premises, finishing up paperwork, perhaps, or getting ready for next year's classes.

The county high school was a nondescript one-story brick building, built in the early Seventies. Charles, who had been sent away to school by his education-conscious parents, had never been on the premises before, but he didn't suppose that it could be too difficult to find a science teacher in that sprawling maze of corridors. After all, students manage to get from one class to another in five minutes. A sign beside the front doors said VISITORS REPORT TO MAIN OFFICE.

Charles followed the arrows down the hall, wondering what he would say when he got there.

The school secretary, a plump, pleasant-looking woman who resembled the mother character in a Forties movie, motioned him over to the office counter with a friendly smile. "May I help you?"

"Yes," said Charles. "I'm looking for your physics teacher." He had decided not to explain unless he had to.

"Physics. That would be Mr. Worthington. Go down the hall—"

"Does he also teach chemistry?" asked Charles, who didn't want to speak to *Mr.* Anybody.

"That's right."

"How about biology?" asked Charles.

"No. That's Miss Aynsley."

Charles breathed a sigh of relief. "That's the one!" Seeing the puzzled look on the secretary's face, he hastened to add, "I'm a reporter for *Scholastic Science*." He beamed at her, pleased with the name of his newly invented magazine. "I'm doing a feature on science in Georgia schools, and I'm speaking to various teachers."

The secretary looked doubtful.

Everybody's suspicious of the media these days, thought Charles. "Miss Aynsley has been recommended to us as one of the best teachers," he said heartily.

The woman's brow cleared. "Well, that's all right, then," she said. "You go down the hall—"

Charles followed her directions, hurrying out of embarrassment and anticipation. He noticed that on the cinderblock wall beside each door, a hand-lettered sign identified the teacher within. He found the MISS AYNSLEY sign in a matter of minutes, and its decoration of frogs and butterflies told him that indeed she did teach biology.

He wondered what he was going to say to her when he found her. Should he pretend to interview her for a nonexistent magazine, just in case she checked with the secretary? He didn't have time to consider the question any more, because someone was coming toward him, making it awkward for him to be loitering in the hall. Taking a deep breath, Charles strolled into the classroom and said, "I'm looking for Miss Aynsley."

"Yes, young man? What can I do for you?"

She was a hundred if she was a day. She had been weaned on a pickle. She probably *ate* the frogs after the class dissected them. Charles stood frozen in his tracks contemplating the most vinegary old martinet he had ever encountered.

"Yes?" she said again.

"I'm sorry," said Charles. "I came to ask you what phylum earthworms are in, but I have just remembered."

The same one I'm *in*, he finished silently, hurrying down the hall toward the exit.

◆   ◆   ◆

WESLEY ROUNTREE COULDN'T help thinking how incongruous the setting was. Here they were in a formal Colonial-style living room, with a grand piano and green velvet drapes, and a cream-colored Oriental carpet. Against one wall an oak sideboard held an assortment of silver and crystal ornaments—that must be the wedding-present display, he thought—but here on the marble-topped coffee table was a mound of human remains. He wouldn't like to have to explain this to the lady of the house. In that event Wesley doubted if he'd get a word in edgewise.

This wasn't exactly his idea of an expert witness, either: a girl who looked hardly more than a teenager, wearing jeans and an oversized sweatshirt. He had to admit, though, that despite the unusual nature of the surroundings, the information provided had been fast and was confidently given. The sheriff was inclined to trust the opinions offered, but he wasn't planning to go into detail with anyone about where he had obtained them.

"So these remains are human," said Wesley, when Elizabeth had given her verdict. "I was afraid of that.

What did you mean, though, that I got more than I bargained for? Who is it?"

Elizabeth sighed and shook her head. "The Mormon Tabernacle Choir?" she suggested.

Wesley blinked. "Come again?"

"I mean, there are traces of more than one body in here, Sheriff."

"What, that little bit of ash is more than one person? It hardly seems like enough."

"I don't think you have the ashes of a complete body here," Elizabeth told him. "You're right: there aren't enough ashes to indicate that multiple bodies were put into the urn. But I don't think this sampling is *all* of *anybody*. You have bits and pieces of several. Look here: this is a porcelain tooth from a partial plate, and these are fragments of teeth that are badly decayed, and *this* is a baby tooth! Also, this big bit of bone here is the epiphysis of a femur, and there is some indication of arthritis, but *this* bone is from a younger individual. In fact, I'd say this smaller one is from a female."

Wesley stared at the evidence, trying to make sense of the new information. "Are you sure about this?"

Elizabeth nodded. "Even if I were a complete klutz when it came to bone analysis, *nobody* could be wrong about one particular bit of evidence here. Look at this." She held out a handful of metal brackets of two different sizes. "What do you make of that?"

"Can't place them," said the sheriff. "Not tooth fillings?"

"They're staples," said Elizabeth, grinning triumphantly. "You see, there are two basic kinds of cremation. There's a deluxe plan, in which the deceased is placed in a pine casket to be incinerated, and then there's the economy funeral, which uses a container which is more or less . . . cardboard. Now, these big staples fastened the pine box together and the little ones came from the cardboard casket."

"So we know that the remains here come from at least two funerals."

"At least two. Probably more." Elizabeth looked extremely pleased with herself. "I learned all this from a medical examiner in North Carolina. He came up to the university to talk to us about his cases. One of his strangest tasks was to identify the remains when a funeral home accidentally sent the wrong urns to the families of the deceased and the medical examiner had to sort them out."

Wesley was still stunned into silence. "This takes some getting used to," he said at last. "I was prepared for murder, but this—"

"Murder?" Elizabeth's eyes widened. "Oh, you don't have to worry about *murder*, Sheriff Rountree. Fraud maybe, but certainly nothing violent."

"Fraud?"

"Sure. When a body is cremated, not all the ash gets

collected and put into an urn. A few stray bits and pieces stay behind in the grate of the incinerator, and after a number of cremations, that grate has to be removed and cleaned out." She pointed to the pile of ashes on the newspaper. "What I think you have here is—"

Wesley nodded. "Somebody cleaned out the grate and dumped the leftovers into that urn."

"That'd be my guess," Elizabeth agreed. "Ship it off to Atlanta to be sure, though."

"Oh, I will," Wesley assured her. "First thing tomorrow. So the question now is: where did these remains come from?"

"I can't help you there." She picked up the blue enamel vase and examined it carefully. "I take it you've looked at this?"

Wesley nodded. "Sure. Fingerprinted it, too."

"Usually, funeral homes put serial numbers on their urns, and they have number codes so that they can tell which urns are theirs. This one is blank, though. I suppose there are other places one could obtain one. You say it was mailed to the widow from California?"

"She thought so," grunted Wesley. "Says she never checked the wrapping to find out."

"Well, that's understandable. She was in mourning, after all."

"She's over it now from the look of her," the sheriff remarked. "I'd say if that husband of hers staged a third coming, she'd arrange his next departure personally."

"There's no chance of that, is there?"

"No. This time I called California myself, and they faxed me a photo of the deceased. This time around it's official."

"Wonder what happened last time," mused Elizabeth.

"Emmet Mason left home, saying he was going to California." Wesley ticked off the facts one by one on his fingers. "His wife gets a phone call from somebody saying he's dead. To corroborate this report of his death, she receives a funeral urn, supposedly containing Emmet, but actually filled with—" Wesley made a face.

"Leftovers," suggested Elizabeth.

"So somebody provided Emmet Mason with a perfect way out. No messy divorce, no recriminations. As far as Chandler Grove, Georgia, is concerned, Emmet is dead. But instead of going to heaven, he went to California."

"Some people would consider that the other alternative."

This remark brought Wesley Rountree back to full alert and he decided that he should not be sitting around theorizing with a civilian, expert witness or no. "I want to thank you for your time," he said sol-

emnly, scooping the evidence back into its container.
"You certainly have been helpful."

"You're welcome," said Elizabeth. "And any other
time, I'd love to be of any help I could to you in
solving this case, but I'm getting married next week.
I just don't have time to get involved."

Wesley's eyes twinkled. "I think I can take it from
here," he said gravely.

CHAPTER

10

DEPUTY CLAY TAYLOR arrived at the sheriff's department at 7:53 A.M. to find the coffeepot on and a note on his desk from Wesley Rountree, giving him instructions for the day's interrogations. Wesley himself, the note explained, had gone off to court. After that he proposed to drive directly out to question the proprietor of the regional crematorium. He had no plans to return to the office in between. In his absence, the deputy was to attempt to ascertain the number of local residents who had been cremated within the last seven years.

"How does he expect me to do that?" grunted Clay in disgust. "Go door-to-door?"

Two cups of coffee later he had given the matter enough thought to figure out how to proceed. The logical person to begin with would be Azzie Todd, manager of Todd and O'Connor Funeral Home in Chandler Grove. He had learned from his telephone inquiries that their firm did not do cremations, but Clay felt that they could advise him on what steps to take next. What he did *not* want was to look up every obituary in the local newspaper for the last seven years and then contact each family individually.

With some misgivings about the nature of his errand, the deputy set out for the funeral home. Like most Southern mortuaries, the Chandler Grove establishment had begun its existence as a large private home. It stood on Main Street, white-columned and splendid, with spreading oak trees and a perfectly manicured lawn. Its former owners had become customers of Todd and O'Connor too long ago for anyone to remember or care that the house had once been a happier, if less tidy, place.

After a brisk walk out of the business district and into the tree-lined old section of Main Street, Clay found himself outside the wrought-iron fence of Todd and O'Connor, wondering how to conduct the inquiry. Naturally they would want to know why he was asking such questions—and since the perpetrator of the fraud had not been determined, the deputy wasn't sure that he should tell them.

He hurried up the cement walk to the freshly painted gray porch and prepared to ring the bell. The door was ajar. *They probably don't like a lot of noise here,* thought Clay, *And it's not as if anyone would come here to steal anything.*

He had been inside a number of times before, but never alone, and he would have been ashamed to admit how uneasy he felt at doing so now. It was the deputy's experience that people usually went to funerals in groups. He supposed that law enforcement officers in larger districts would have become quite accustomed to death after a few years on the job, but in rural Georgia, murder was no everyday occurrence. Clay had seen enough car wrecks to last him a lifetime, but mercifully few victims of homicide.

As soon as he entered the oak-paneled hallway, a solemn young man in a gray suit materialized from an inner sanctum and in hushed tones inquired whether he could be of help. The boy could have done with less hair grease and more Clearasil, in Clay's opinion.

"I'd like to see Mr. Todd," he said in his normal

tone of voice. The words seemed to bounce off the walls. "I'm here on official business."

With a cordial nod, the apparition scuttled back into the offices, and Clay could hear the murmur of lowered voices discussing his arrival. Clay studied the Victorian prints on display in the hall. Todd and O'Connor seemed to favor Landseer animal portraits, along the lines of *The Old Shepherd Is Mourned by His Canine Companion*. The artist had a way with animals: their expressions made them almost seem human.

The deputy felt the presence of someone behind him and turned so quickly that he almost collided with the velvety person of Azzie Todd. Everything about the funeral director was sleek and molelike, and he had an unfortunate shortsighted gaze over a pointed snout that completed the image. He reminded Clay of the children's book *Wind in the Willows*. Idly, the deputy wondered if Mr. O'Connor completed the firm's literary allusion by resembling a large and aristocratic toad.

He ushered the deputy into a small back office with earth-tone walls (*the burrow*, thought Clay, fighting to keep a straight face). After he had seated himself behind a cluttered antique desk, Mr. Todd folded his hands primly and asked what he could do for the local constabulary.

"I am conducting an inquiry," said Clay, answering

the formality in kind. "And I need some information—or at least, your advice on how I can obtain it."

"And that is?"

"I need to know whether anyone was cremated in this county in the last seven years, and if so who. And *by* whom."

Concern flickered across Azzie Todd's talpine features. "We at Todd and O'Connor don't offer that service," he said.

"I know. This investigation would have been a whole lot easier if you did."

The funeral director looked puzzled. "Has there been a murder?"

"Why do you ask that?" asked Clay, thinking that murder had been a strange, and perhaps telling, conclusion to reach on the basis of his question.

Todd blushed. "I read detective stories. Cremation is the ideal way to conceal your crime. You poison someone and then have them cremated. No evidence!"

The deputy considered it. "Lord, I hope we don't have that to contend with. At the moment, it's more like a case of mistaken identity. I really can't be any more specific than that."

"I understand," said Todd, making a steeple with his fingertips. "Discretion is a byword with us."

"On the phone the other day, I believe you said

that you farm out any cremation requests, so to speak. Would you have a list of any such cases?"

"No. Why should we? Anyway, it doesn't happen very often. Seven years? I can go back twenty. We've had three such requests. One was the Hadley boy, who moved out to the West Coast and left instructions in his will that he was to be cremated. His parents didn't much care for the idea, but they did it anyway."

"Was the body cremated here in Georgia?"

"No. Done there, and the ashes mailed here. We made the arrangements by telephone with a firm out there. The second was one of those commune people—Earthling, I think they call their company. One of the fellows out there died in a car wreck and the rest decided to cremate the body and to scatter the ashes in their meadow. I referred them to Elijah's Chariot, as I always do in these cases, but I must say I did suspect them of doing it out of stinginess. He left them all his money; they spent less than five hundred dollars on his funeral. That young man was an heir to some minor tobacco fortune." He shook his head in wonder that this was so. "Ever noticed that most of these hippie types that want to live on the land come from well-to-do families?"

"Sure," said Clay, no stranger to that lifestyle himself. "If poor kids want to eat beans and sleep on the floor, they can stay home and do it. Do you remember the name of the deceased?"

"Christopher Greene. They called him something else, though. Rama-something."

The deputy made a note of it. "Now didn't you say that there was a third case?"

"That I know of, yes," said Todd. "Now, you understand there may be people in the community who take their business elsewhere without consulting me. In order to be absolutely certain, I think you'll have to check the death records at the courthouse one at a time."

Clay grimaced at the unwelcome suggestion. He was afraid that such a chore might be inevitable. "And the third was . . ."

"Jeter Wales. He was at least eighty and his nearest kinfolks were some first cousin's children in Ohio, so they—"

The deputy wrote down the name. "I don't think that's who I'm looking for."

"That's about all I know to tell you," said Azzie Todd with a mournful smile. "You really want to go to the courthouse and check those death records."

Clay Taylor sighed. "No, I don't. Want to, I mean."

◆ ◆ ◆

ELIZABETH MACPHERSON had seldom been more cheerful at breakfast. She smiled when asked to pass the sugar bowl; she made bright and inane conversation to no one in particular; and she kept taking deep breaths as if she were about to burst into song. Geoffrey was afraid she would. Driven from his bed by the sound of the vacuum cleaner in the upstairs hall, he had crept to the table in stupefied silence, where he had attempted to ingest a cup of black coffee without attracting undue attention.

As usual, Captain Grandfather and Dr. Chandler were nowhere to be seen, having breakfasted at seven, and Aunt Amanda was supervising the cleaning operations. Charles, screened from view by the Atlanta newspaper he was reading, had coffee and a cup of yogurt in front of him, which he would attempt to reach with his spoon from time to time without lowering the paper. It was a bit like watching a robot arm handle radioactive substances. This, unfortunately, left no one for Elizabeth to be pleasant to except a comatose Geoffrey.

"Isn't it a lovely morning?" she asked, beaming in his general direction.

Geoffrey's expression suggested that he considered the two terms mutually exclusive.

"I called Miss Grey, the dressmaker, yesterday, and she has promised to do the dresses. I have an appointment with her this afternoon, to be measured and so on. I must call Jenny and see if she can go as well."

"I take it that no atrocities are planned for the male

hostages in this event?" asked Geoffrey. "Not kilts or anything?"

"No, Geoffrey. Just don't wear your velvet cloak."

He managed a taut smile. "I am saving that for my visit to you in Edinburgh—when you are the Lady Elizabeth."

She sighed. "That sounds awfully nice, doesn't it? Unfortunately it's impossible."

"Is Cameron not knighthood material, then?"

"I have no idea," said the bride-to-be. "But even if he's knighted, I wouldn't be Lady Elizabeth. If he becomes Sir Cameron, I would be Lady *Dawson*, and if *I* received a knighthood, I'd be *Dame* Elizabeth. The only women who can use *lady* before their first names are the daughters of earls. Or dukes."

"Like Lady Diana?"

"Yes. And, by the way, the same thing applies to the term *princess*. I know that the Princess of Wales is called Princess Diana, but that is not correct. She is Lady Diana—because she is the daughter of the Earl of Spencer—or she is the Princess of Wales. But not Princess Diana. Only the Princess Anne is entitled to use the title before her given name." Elizabeth sighed. "Titles are not easy to come by. Anyway, I'll never be Lady Elizabeth: I had the wrong parents."

"At the risk of prompting another lecture out of Debrett, may I wish your bridegroom a knighthood?" said Geoffrey courteously.

From the recesses of the front hall, the doorbell chimed. "Oh, dear!" cried Elizabeth. "I hope that isn't the sheriff again!" She set her napkin beside her plate and hurried to answer the door.

Geoffrey took advantage of this blessed interruption to draw the curtains to the French windows and to pour himself another cup of coffee.

Charles peered over the top of the newspaper and pushed his own empty cup out for a refill. "What did she mean, she hopes it's not the sheriff? What is she up to?"

"When I awaken, I shall ask her," Geoffrey promised.

They sipped their coffee in companionable silence for a few moments until Elizabeth returned. "Postman," she announced, still beaming. "He brought another wedding present. Huge box—I could barely lift it. From New York. It's addressed to *Cameron Dawson and Fiancée*, though, so I've left it until he gets here. Probably one of his marine-biologist cronies. Just think, Cameron will be here in four days!" She clapped her hands in glee, much to her cousins' disgust.

Geoffrey crumpled his napkin and threw it up in the air.

"Oh, by the way, Charles," said Elizabeth, pushing down the top of his newspaper and ignoring the ensuing scowl. "There was also a letter for you. From *Snow White?*"

Charles stifled a cough. "Just a little joke," he muttered, snatching the letter. He hurried out of the room before anyone could comment further.

Elizabeth stared after him. "What is he up to?"

"We were just about to ask you the same thing," Geoffrey replied. "What was that remark of yours about hoping the sheriff hadn't come back?"

"He was consulting me about a case," said Elizabeth in her grandest manner. "Forensic anthropology."

"Wesley Rountree has a *case*? What is it? Chicken thieves?"

"No, Geoffrey. It involves fraud and people pretending to be dead. I had to identify cremated remains."

Geoffrey snickered. "I assure you, cousin, that anyone who has been cremated is not merely *pretending* to be dead."

Elizabeth was so stung by this mocking interruption of her serious (and self-congratulatory) discussion that she explained the entire case to him in the haughty tones of an expert witness. She told him about Emmet Mason's second demise, and about the mixture of bodies in the cremation urn, emphasizing her own skills as a forensic anthropologist in identifying the mysterious remains. "I told Miss Grey about it on the telephone when I called about my dress. She had read the engagement announcement in the paper, and so she knew that I was an anthropologist. She said that it was wonderful how clever girls of my generation are. She's quite right! I was brilliant," she assured him. "But of course, I shan't take any further interest in the matter," she declared. "Because I'm getting married next week, which is much more important."

Geoffrey looked thoughtful. "It is an interesting case, though," he murmured.

◆ ◆ ◆

WESLEY ROUNTREE SUPPOSED that there could be worse names for a crematorium than Elijah's Chariot, Inc. Other biblical titles might be even more unfortunate: Shadrach, Meshach, and Abednego's, for example, which would be an oblique reference to the fiery furnace of Old Testament fame. Or maybe Lot's Wife and Company—after the lady in Genesis who was turned into a pillar of salt in a sort of divine and instantaneous cremation. Wesley felt that names could be a tricky matter in a business like that. Any suggestion of the flames of hell and your business would go right up in smoke.

Still, it made him suspicious, and he was very interested in meeting the joker who had given such an unusual name to a most uncommon business. He had thought about it all morning as he sat in court waiting to testify in the reckless-driving case. Strictly speaking, he supposed that he ought to notify the law enforcement agency of the county he was going to, but he doubted that they'd want to be bothered. There was not as yet any evidence that a crime involving their jurisdiction had taken place. At this point Wesley figured that he was just on a fishing trip: questioning a witness who might or might not be involved. If it turned out later that he was involved, then Wesley would tip off Wayne Dupree, sheriff of Roan County, and turn the case over to him. Right now he just wanted some answers.

He enjoyed the drive on the corkscrew county roads, and the view of rolling meadows and the green mountains thick with hardwoods. He was far enough back in the hills now so that there weren't any cute subdivisions with names like Brook Valley edging out the pastureland. He wondered why a crematorium should be so far out in the country. *So as not to make the neighbors nervous,* he told himself. He slipped a Statler Brothers cassette into the tape deck and sang along, enjoying the sunshine and the beauty of a June day in the hills of Georgia; but in the back of his mind a list of questions was forming.

◆　◆　◆

CLARINE MASON fingered the crystal pendant around her neck and took three deep breaths. She really *was* feeling better. It was quite amazing. The pendant was absorbing all her negative feelings, just like they said it would. Perhaps the herbal tea had been a help, too. She resolved to buy more of it; after all, they had been kind to her and they needed the business, and after all, ginseng really might be an anti-depressant.

Clarine poured hot water into the teapot and waited for the herbs to steep. The kitchen was sunny and comforting in the morning light. She felt happy to be on her own among her plants and her cross-stitched samplers. She was all right in the kitchen; it was the parlor that bothered her, with that blatant bare spot on the mantel that used to be a memorial to Emmet.

She had wanted to talk to somebody about her anger and her sense of humiliation at Emmet's betrayal, but as she considered her friends one by one, she could find no one in whom she wanted to confide. Most of her friends were older women like herself, and although they would never admit it, her plight would make them uncomfortable. Somewhere, she thought, under their professions of sympathy, there would be a spark of satisfaction that this had happened to her. That the humiliation had been meted out to her, and not to them. That she was gullible to have believed in Emmet's death in the first place with only a blue jar for proof.

Clarine had thought she'd go crazy that afternoon,

pacing around the big empty house with all that rage building up inside her. But then as she was tidying up the kitchen, she'd noticed an old edition of the *Chandler Grove Scout* under a pile of vegetable peelings, and there had been an ad at the bottom of the page.

Treat Your Worries with Nature's Remedies, the ad advised. *Spiritual and Nutritional Counselors at Earthling Will Help You Fight the Blues*. The directions in the ad described the old gristmill by the river as the headquarters of the health-food store and meditation center.

Clarine though to herself, *Well, why not?* She knew about Earthling from local gossip among the ladies' church group. Everyone said that they were a bunch of hippies from out west who believed in eating peculiar food, and who took an interest in political causes that nobody else had ever heard of. Clarine knew all that. But their ad promised help to people with worries. Clarine decided that in this case their being outsiders was a point in their favor. Telling her troubles to those crazy people would hardly count as disclosure. It wasn't as if anybody who *mattered* would find out. In fact, she thought, considering the peculiarities of their own lifestyles, they were hardly in any position to look down on her for being a discarded wife.

The potions of Earthling, Inc., seemed to Clarine to be her best chance of consolation without confiding in her friends and neighbors, those whose esteem she valued. Heaven forbid that Dr. Chandler should learn about the shame of Emmet's defection. She would much rather try the mumbo jumbo of a bunch of raggedy strangers than confide in her lifelong acquaintances.

In a mood of desperation, gambling on a long shot, Clarine had gone to visit Earthling. When she reached the old gristmill, she parked the car in the gravel lot. Inside the cluttered shop, she looked around as if she were a casual tourist, trying not to attract any undue attention. She was nervous, not knowing what to expect from these outlandish strangers, and she was bewildered by all the strange and unpronounceable items they sold.

Just as she was ready to dash from the shop and forget the whole thing, a dark-haired woman in braids and an Indian print dress appeared and asked her if she'd like some tea. She seemed so sincere about the offer that Clarine forgot to say no, and soon she was sitting in the back room telling her life story to Shanti, which is what the girl said to call her. Shanti had seemed most interested in Emmet's return from the ashes, as it were. But she said that since death was only a state of mind anyway, that Clarine should feel perfectly free to count Emmet's first death as the valid one for psychic purposes. Just forget this little epilogue, she'd advised. After two more cups of tea, she and Shanti were in perfect agreement that Emmet had racked up enough bad karma to come back as a cock-roach, and that Clarine was not to worry about any loose ends that Emmet had left in his new life. Shanti prescribed herbal tea and a healing crystal, and she urged Clarine to come back for meditation classes.

Clarine decided that she'd go to Earthling's pro-grams on Tuesdays and Thursdays. That way, it wouldn't conflict with ladies' circle on Monday and Wednesday-night choir practice. She poured herself a cup of herbal tea and added two spoonfuls of sugar. She was feeling much better indeed now that she was busy. Emmet was already fading from her conscious-ness like a bad dream.

The telephone rang, startling her so much that she spilled a few drops of tea. Setting the cup down care-fully in its saucer, she hurried to answer it.

"Mrs. Clarine Mason?" said another of those plastic West Coast voices.

"Oh, Lord God! What is it *this* time?" cried Clarine, completely out of patience with intrusions from Cal-ifornia.

"I'm with the coroner's office, ma'am, and I'm look-ing at this form here on your late husband Mr. Emmet J. Mason, and I see that the officer who called you has neglected to put down what you'd like us to do with your late husband's remains—"

In words of one syllable, Clarine told him.

◆ ◆ ◆

"I DON'T CARE IF you're Wyatt Earp," said Susan Davis in her sternest voice. "You can't bring that Co-Cola in here. There are irreplaceable documents in this office. So you either dump it out, or you stay outside the railing until you finish it."

"Aw, Sue," moaned Clay Taylor. "Come on. I have a couple of hours' work to do, and I'll probably even miss lunch. It's police business," he added for good measure.

Susan Davis was not impressed. "Parking tickets is police business," she observed. "That don't mean you get to break the rules in here and get me in trouble with Mrs. Horne." Her dark eyes flashed as she made her pronouncement and she went back to copying names in a record book.

With a sigh of resignation, Clay Taylor returned to the basement hall of the courthouse and finished his drink. He wondered how anybody as pretty as Susan Davis could be in such a perpetually bad mood. She had beautiful dark hair, worn long, except for a bit at the front caught up in a barrette, and her features were cameo perfect. If it weren't for the perpetual snarl, she could be lovely. Her face in repose was a frown of disapproval and she could wring vinegar out of the most sugary comments addressed to her. In the three years during which Clay had been a deputy, he had occasion to encounter Susan at least once a week on visits to the records office, and he had yet to observe her in a good mood. There wasn't much point in arguing with her, though, he thought, taking another swallow of Coke. He just hoped that someday Miss Dragon Lady would do 56 m.p.h. when he was out with the radar gun.

In a few minutes he reappeared at the counter of the records office. "Will you let me in now?"

Susan's expression suggested that he was still a nuisance, but that she would have to put up with him. She opened the wooden barrier and motioned him in. "What do you want?" she asked in tones suggesting complete indifference.

"I need to see the death records in the county for the last five or six years. Can I use your computer?"

Her frown deepened. "No, you can't use my computer. I have work to do! And besides those records haven't been put on disk yet."

"Why not?" asked Clay without thinking.

"Because I'm too busy to get around to it, what with people coming in and wasting my time asking stupid questions!"

"Well, where are the records then?"

"In a drawer, of course! Come on, I'll show you where it is." Her expression suggested that this would involve a four-hour trek through a swamp. In fact they ended up no more than twenty feet from Susan's desk.

She jerked the file drawer open for him and started to stalk away.

"What if somebody lived in this county, but didn't die here?"

She gave him a withering glare. "Then they won't be here, will they?"

"But the obituaries would be in the newspaper," said Clay, thinking aloud.

"That's not my problem!" said Susan, going back to her desk.

"Okay, I'll check here first, and then look in the archives at the *Scout* office."

"Bully for you."

Clay began to examine the death records for 1985. He wondered if Susan's personality would change when she was no longer young and pretty, or if her nearest and dearest were already looking into untraceable poisons.

◆ ◆ ◆

ELIJAH'S CHARIOT, INC., was a modest-looking building of whitewashed cinder block set in a field among boxwood shrubs and cedar trees. One white Nissan hatchback was parked on the circular gravel driveway. There were no other cars in sight. Wesley supposed that the business would require only part-time help, if that, and that one person would be sufficient to mind the store. They didn't seem to be too busy today. He noted with relief that no smoke was issuing from the vent pipe in the roof.

Wesley parked his sheriff's car behind the Nissan and went in search of the proprietor. Since it was a place of business, Wesley decided that it would be unnecessary to knock at the front door. He eased it open and went in, calling out, "Hello? Anybody here?"

The front room was an ordinary office. There was an old wooden desk and office fixtures on one side of the room, and the other side contained couches and Queen Anne chairs, much like a doctor's waiting room. The waiting-room walls were decorated with landscapes in the Starving Artist school of hasty realism, while the office portion of the premises was adorned with framed travel posters. A brass plate on the desk announced it to be the domain of Jasper Willis, but Mr. Willis was not in any state to receive visitors. Judging from the amount of blood on the floor beside him, Mr. Willis had just become a prospective client for his own services.

"Well, damn!" said Wesley. He pulled out his handkerchief and draped it over the telephone receiver as he lifted it. "Now I've *got* to get Wayne Dupree in on this case, and he'll probably make me come testify in court for him. Pigheaded so-and-so. Hello, this is Sheriff Wesley Rountree here, from over in Chandler

Grove. Let me speak to your sheriff, please. Wayne? That you, good buddy? Great to talk to you!"

❖ ❖ ❖

IN THE PRIVACY OF his bedroom, Charles Chandler stared at the letter as if he were afraid it might explode. Finally, after days of silence, the lovely blonde from the *Highlander* ad had answered his letter. He was almost afraid to open it. He didn't suppose that anyone would waste a twenty-five-cent stamp just to tell him to go to blazes. How odd, he thought, that even though this was an essentially financial transaction on his part, he still had the pounding heart and sweaty palms of a lovesick adolescent. There was barely a week left until the wedding.

"I hope she's desperate," he muttered, opening the letter.

It was written in ink, in that rounded handwriting that young women usually outgrow before they are thirty. She wasn't lying about her age, he decided. There was no return address or phone number given, he noticed, but all the same it didn't seem to be a rejection. The lady was wary. Charles decided that she was wise to be cautious, considering the nature of the communication. After all, anybody could buy a magazine and answer the ads. He thought that she would be wise not to answer letters postmarked Leavenworth or San Quentin. Charles read the letter through twice, once for content and once for clues.

Dear Charles Chandler,

This is a reply to the letter that you sent to Snow White at the Highlander *magazine.*

Since there aren't too many people in this region, I thought I'd know every person who answered my ad, at least by name, but I've never heard of you. (Are you related to Geoffrey Chandler, by any chance?) And you didn't say whether you worked around here, or what you did. At first I thought it might be some kind of alias or a joke from one of my friends, but your letter sounded sweet, and I decided to answer it anyway.

If this does turn out to be a practical joke, I'll be very mad.

Shouldn't you tell me more about who you really are? Well, never mind. I was very interested to hear that you are a scientest [Charles winced at the spelling] *and although we seem to have rather different interests, you certainly sound like a nice enough person. I have decided that it wouldn't do any harm to meet you, and see if we hit it off. I'm kind of busy right now (as ever!), but I could manage to meet you for a drink at Bubba's in Milton's Forge. If that is all right with you, meet me there at seven Wednesday evening at the bar.*

Since I'm still not sure that this isn't a joke, I don't believe I'll tell you who I am until I see you. But I do hope you are for real.

I'll see you Wednesday, then, at Bubba's, if you decide to go through with this. I'll be wearing a white jacket with a rose on the lapel and carrying an umbrella.

See you soon, I hope!

Snow White

CHAPTER

II

IF SHERIFF WAYNE Dupree was delighted to see his friend and colleague from the neighboring county, he managed to conceal it with admirable restraint. After receiving the unexpected summons from Wesley Rountree, he had dispatched the mobile crime lab and set out for the crematorium, where he intended to get some answers as to what Wesley thought he was doing discovering dead bodies in someone else's jurisdiction.

He found Sheriff Rountree sitting in his patrol car on the gravel driveway, listening to a Statler Brothers tape. Motioning for his men to cordon off the crime scene and get to work, Wayne Dupree ambled over to Rountree's patrol car to discuss the situation.

"'Afternoon, Wayne," said Wesley amiably. "You gonna read me my rights? I got my Miranda card here if you'd like to borrow it."

Wayne Dupree's frown deepened. "You wanna tell me what's going on here?" he growled. It was his opinion that Wesley Rountree was almost as clever as he thought he was. This combination of arrogance and cunning always made Wayne a little uneasy. He suspected Wesley of being up to something at nearly every encounter they had, be it sheriff's-association politics or a jurisdictional dispute over a suspect.

Wesley Rountree was mildness itself. "Honest to Pete, Wayne," he said, holding up a hand in protest, "I just drove over here to question this individual. I didn't even have the notion of getting a warrant—and arrest was definitely not on my agenda. To tell you the truth, I'm not even sure I have a crime." He looked thoughtful. "Well, I guess I'm sure now, considering what happened to my witness."

"He was dead when you got here."

Wesley nodded. "Cold. Rigor mortis was passing

off. I had to check to see if he was beyond help, but other than that I didn't disturb anything. I called you and walked right out."

Wayne Dupree was looking anxiously toward the cinderblock building, where his investigators were performing their tasks.

Wesley looked sympathetic. "You want to go over there and see what's going on, Wayne? I'll go with you."

"Yeah, but you haven't told me—"

"I'll tell you while we watch," said Wesley soothingly.

"Good," grunted the older sheriff. "They can fingerprint you while they're at it."

They made their way to the waiting-room side of the crematorium office, where they could observe the bustle of activity without being in anyone's way. Wesley carefully explained the events of the past few days to an increasingly skeptical Wayne Dupree.

". . . And that's about it," Wesley concluded with a sigh. "I reckon if Emmet Mason had had enough common sense to use a fake name once he got out there to California, none of this would have happened. He could have just died as John Smith, or whoever he wanted to be, and nobody here would ever have known the difference. I guess he must have kept his old Georgia driver's license for sentimental reasons.

Or maybe he wanted to make sure he'd get back home when the time came."

Sheriff Dupree shook his head in disapproval. "What about the insurance money?"

"The money his widow received five years ago, you mean?" asked Wesley. "That has pretty well stumped our insurance agent, let me tell you. He is not used to complexities of this nature. The way he figures it, she wasn't entitled to the money because her husband wasn't dead, but by the time they discovered the fraud, her husband was dead, so they would owe her the money after all. He practically had smoke coming out of his ears by then, so I told him to call the home office in Atlanta and ask them to put one of their company lawyers on the case."

"Was the wife in on the fraud?"

"No, indeed. She's madder than a scalded cat."

"So you think this establishment here provided the ashes that helped perpetrate the fraud?"

"Well, I had to ask," said Wesley. "I didn't see how Emmet Mason could have known anybody in California who would fix him up with a fake urn, unless those folks advertise in magazines, which doesn't seem likely and doesn't bear thinking about."

"The fact that somebody murdered old Jasper seems to confirm your suspicions," Wayne Dupree admitted.

"Yeah, that's what I thought. Who was this Jasper Willis anyhow?"

They turned and looked at the form in the dark suit, presently being outlined in chalk.

"Oh, he's local," said the sheriff. "I didn't know him too well, of course. My county is bigger than yours." He smirked.

Wesley thought up a rude reply, but did not say it.

"His dad owned a big funeral home downtown, which he left to his two sons: Jasper and the older boy, Jared. That's the brother I'm acquainted with. He does a lot of civic work. Jared Willis is a good man, knows his business, pillar of the community, but Jasper was just so much dead wood. Didn't want to go into the funeral business. Couldn't seem to make a go of a regular job. Finally, Jared Willis got the idea of investing in a crematorium to service the whole region. He knew it wouldn't make much money now—might even be a tax loss, he told me once—but he figured that in case the environmentalist movement really caught on here, the place could become profitable in ten years or so."

"Maybe so," said Wesley politely.

"Meanwhile, he put Jasper out here to run it, with some help from the other mortuary employees on an as-needed basis. There wasn't a lot to do, so Jasper couldn't make too much of a mess of things." The sheriff looked again at the crime scene and frowned. "Apparently, though, he managed to do it, anyhow."

Wesley digested this information. "Say, Wayne," he said thoughtfully, "you said Jasper didn't want to be a funeral director. Do you have any idea what he did want to be?"

Sheriff Dupree considered it. "Nothing sinister," he said at last. "Not like drugs or racing stock cars, or anything. Let's see, what was it?" He looked at the office, and suddenly his face cleared. "I've got it! He wanted to be a travel agent."

Wesley nodded. "You know, Wayne, I believe he was."

◆ ◆ ◆

VISITORS TO CHANDLER GROVE were often a bit disconcerted to learn that the Grey House was actually a bright yellow Colonial with green shutters, but the locals would explain to them that the name of the house referred to its owners rather than to its physical attributes.

It had been built around 1930 by Dr. Sanford Grey, at that time the only physician in the county. He had made house calls at all hours of the day or night, braving the red clay roads on a large bay mare named Daisy, who was more reliable on uncertain terrain than the cars of that era. The doctor had accepted payment for his services in hams and fresh eggs, if need be. Somehow, despite these sacrifices, he had managed to become quite wealthy, and he had married well, which is always useful, if one happens to be of a charitable nature in business. Dr. Grey and his wealthy but mousy wife Evangeline had built a grand and spacious house and raised two daughters, neither of whom ever married, though perhaps for different reasons. Local gossip had it that Miss Geneva was too shy to be courted, and Miss Aurelia was too fierce to be wanted.

In the Forties the teenaged sisters went away to a genteel girls' school—and then came home again. Miss Geneva had acquired expert instruction in fine sewing, a collection of Victorian poetry, and the ability to play the complete works of Stephen Foster on the piano. The only oversight in her otherwise well-spent four years was neglect in finding a husband, but, as she seemed disinclined to remedy the matter, her parents welcomed her back into the fold, and she resumed her previous duties of sewing and flower arranging as if her mind had not been sullied by Latin verbs and plane geometry.

On the other hand, Miss Aurelia had graduated cum laude with a degree in nursing, much disapproved of by her mother, but at last it was decided that propriety would be served if she only worked as an assistant to her father, where her contacts with the unsavory side of life could presumably be monitored by her ever-watchful parent. What Miss Aurelia thought of this was not discussed outside the family, but those who knew her in later years suspected that the argument had taken place fortissimo and almost entirely in words of Anglo-Saxon derivation. Nevertheless, in this case age and treachery overcame youth and skill, and Aurelia Grey, after discovering that no medical personnel were inclined to hire her (a quiet word from the doctor was always suspected in this matter), she settled into Chandler Grove to serve as her father's assistant. By all accounts, she had been good at her job; indeed, had she belonged to a later generation, she would have become a doctor herself, but unfortunately hers was not to be a lasting career.

In the late Fifties, Dr. Grey died of a heart attack while smoking his third cigar of the evening at the annual church barbecue. By the time the old doctor had passed away, his neurasthenic wife was well on her way to becoming a picturesque invalid. The practice was passed on to other physicians (most notably Robert Chandler), and Miss Aurelia devoted her nursing skills to the care of her mother. Despite Mrs. Grey's delicate constitution (vaguely described to appropriate inquirers as *female trouble*), old Mrs. Grey had managed to live to be eighty-four, thanks perhaps to the devoted nursing of her daughters. When at last she died, Miss Geneva was quite prostrate with grief, while her sister tidied up her mother's legal affairs, parceled out her clothes, and—as soon as she could safely leave her grieving sister—departed for a vacation in Florida.

People thought that it was high time Aurelia Grey had a bit of fun in life, and no one could have been more surprised than Chandler Grove to learn two weeks later that Aurelia herself had died suddenly while visiting the Everglades. All things considered, her sister took the additional loss rather well, and she continued to live on in the house, pursuing her routine of church work and fine sewing just as she had before. Everyone said they would have thought that Miss Geneva would be the first to go, being delicate like her mother; but the more progressive town gossips noted that Type-A personalities like Dr. Grey and his eldest daughter were the best bets for an early demise. *Overengined for the beam*, they declared.

By the time she had arrived for a consultation with Miss Geneva Grey, Elizabeth had been thoroughly briefed on the family history, because Southerners believe that who you are has very little to do with present circumstances. Elizabeth had, of course, been instructed to mention none of what she had been told, and indeed, under no circumstances was she to allow the word *Everglades* to be uttered in conversation with Miss Geneva.

She parked her car in the driveway under the oak

tree and was heading up the cement walk toward the front door when a quick blast from a sports-car horn signaled the arrival of the maid of honor. Jenny emerged from her car, looking like a collector doll from the Danbury Mint. Her hair was a confection of spun gold and her scoop-necked garden dress in an English rose pattern looked like formal daywear. *Two sizes larger*, thought Elizabeth, *and I could wear it to the Royal Garden Party. Okay*, three *sizes larger.*

"Isn't this exciting?" cried Jenny in her best Sparkle Plenty voice. "I just love dress fittings! If we had time, I know some places in Atlanta. . . . Oh, but they're a little expensive."

"I'm sure this will be fine," said Elizabeth. "I've brought some material and a pattern, but we can do some alterations in the design, if she's up to it."

Jenny looked at the bride-to-be appraisingly. "Honey, you did pick an A-line, didn't you?"

◆   ◆   ◆

GEOFFREY CHANDLER did not limit his love of drama to the confines of the theatre. Indeed, he felt that the little comedies and melodramas played out in his native village afforded just as much entertainment as anything ever written by the Bard of Avon. Geoffrey was not necessarily inclined to gossip, as he saw no reason to share the best bits with anyone else, but he did enjoy keeping himself informed about the little dramas that were going on about him.

When his cousin Elizabeth had let slip her news about the reprise of Emmet Mason's death scene and the subsequent suspicion that some of the local dearly departed had not gone so far as the hereafter when they exited Chandler Grove, he had resolved to pursue a quiet inquiry of his own. Geoffrey had no desire to be helpful to the police in this matter—or even to share his findings with other interested parties; he simply thought that it would be amusing to know.

"At least it would save one the bother of trying to call them up on the Ouija board, if one learns that they are presently residing in Escondido, California," he remarked to himself. As soon as Elizabeth had left for her dressmaker's appointment, Geoffrey went out to his own car and headed for the one-block section of downtown Chandler Grove.

He decided to forgo a look at the courthouse records. "I wouldn't pass the time of day with Susan Davis to find out if *I* were dead," he muttered.

Five minutes later, he strolled into the office of the *Chandler Grove Scout*, where Marshall Pavlock was hard at work, pasting up the Piggly Wiggly ad. He was a heavyset man with a shock of white hair and a mild expression somewhat at odds with his eyes.

"Hello, Marshall," said Geoffrey, edging past the customers' counter. "Don't let me disturb you."

◆

"I won't," said the editor and owner of the news-paper. "Not unless you've brought an ad about the new playhouse production."

"Not yet," said Geoffrey. *"Ripeness is all."*

Marshall Pavlock frowned. "That's *Lear*. I thought you were doing *Twelfth Night*."

"Well, we are. Oh, never mind. Anyhow I've come about something else." Geoffrey did not enjoy barding to an overeducated audience. It spoiled the spontaneity. "I'd like to look at the back issues of the *Scout*."

The editor looked up from his ad with a puzzled expression. "Is there a scavenger hunt going on in town or something?"

"Why do you ask?"

"You're the second person asking to see those papers. Now ordinarily we don't get more than a dozen requests a year like that, and most of those are from high-school kids. I just wondered why all of a sudden it has become such a popular pastime."

"Who was the other person who asked to see them?"

"The deputy. Clay Taylor. I got the impression from him that it was police business."

"I expect it was," said Geoffrey smoothly. "We probably want to see the papers for entirely different reasons."

"Maybe so," said Marshall. "But if you're onto anything that would be useful as a news story, you let me know about it." He motioned Geoffrey to the back room where the bound copies of the *Scout* were kept.

"Out of my lean and low ability I'll lend you something," muttered Geoffrey, but he took care that Marshall Pavlock should not overhear him.

An hour later Geoffrey emerged from the back room with a notepad full of interesting facts gleaned from the obituary columns of the *Scout*. He did not, however, share his findings with the editor of that publication.

◆ ◆ ◆

ELIZABETH AND JENNY were having tea with Geneva Grey, who had recovered somewhat from her surprise upon meeting them. Or, rather, upon meeting Jenny. She had seemed quite equal to the honor of greeting Elizabeth, but when she had turned to welcome her second visitor, her face registered recognition, shock, and then delight in short order.

"Aren't you—why, you're my weather girl!" she cried, glancing at the television set as if in search of evidence of Jenny's escape.

Jenny Ramsay smiled her demure princess smile, and her eyelids fluttered. "Oh, I can't believe you recognized me!" she murmured. "Aren't you sweet? I'm afraid I look like a dishrag in this old thing."

Miss Grey, a small-boned woman with shining white hair and a dazzling smile of her own, had beamed back at the Weather Princess. "And *you're* getting married!" she exclaimed.

"No, sorry," said Elizabeth, with a little wave of her hand. "Over here. Yes, me. I'm the bride."

The seamstress's smile decreased in voltage ever so slightly. "Well, of course you are!" she said, patting Elizabeth on the arm. "I remember now. You told me all about your bone work on the telephone. It completely slipped my mind when I saw Jenny here. And afterward, you're going to fly over to England and see the Queen."

"Scotland, actually," said Elizabeth, blushing.

"Well, do come in, and let's talk about this exciting event." She cast a last beaming smile at Jenny. "Just wait till I tell folks I had the Channel Four weather girl in for tea!"

She settled them on a faded velvet love seat in the parlor, then she bustled into the kitchen to make the tea. When they were alone, Jenny leaned over to Elizabeth and whispered, "I'm sorry. You must be about ready to kill me!"

Elizabeth summoned up a pale smile. "No, of course not, Jenny. I think it's wonderful for you." Privately she wondered how Jenny Ramsay would look in malarial yellow.

"You know, we never did talk about exactly where

your aunt's house is," said Jenny. "I have to be able
to find it on Saturday, you know!"

"You can't miss it," said Elizabeth. "It's Long
Meadow Farm. There's a Bavarian castle across the
road."

"Oh my," said Jenny, wide-eyed. "Are you related
to *them?*"

"Sure. Amanda Chandler is my mother's sister. In
fact, her sons Charles and Geoffrey are part of the
wedding party. They didn't go to school in Chandler
Grove, though. Did you ever meet them?"

Jenny laughed pleasantly. "I meet so many people,"
she said. "If they ever served on a civic committee,
I'm sure I've crossed paths with them. Are they cute?"

Elizabeth hesitated. "They're . . . interesting."

"Well," said Jenny, "anybody with that much money
is interesting."

Presently, Miss Grey returned, bearing a silver tray
on which a Spode tea service rested in newly rinsed
splendor. Beside it was a plate of home-baked cookies. "Now," she said, beaming at them, "I want to hear
all about it!"

"Well," said Elizabeth, "I'm afraid it's short notice,
because the wedding is only a week away, but I've
been dieting, you see, and—"

"You're not sweet on that Badger Darnell, are
you?"

"I'm sorry," said Elizabeth, losing her train of thought. "What did you say?"

Jenny gave a little cough. "I believe she means me, honey." She directed another princess look at their hostess. "No, ma'am, I'm not at all involved with Badger. Why, I think of him as a big brother, and that's all. He's like family. But he certainly is an eligible bachelor, so if you want him, you go right ahead."

Geneva Grey gave a little squeal of laughter and tapped Jenny playfully on the arm. That line always did go down well with the little old ladies.

Elizabeth took a deep breath and counted to ten. Then she reached for a cookie. "As I said, we have very little time, but I did bring a pattern that you might want to look at." She reached into her totebag and brought out the thick envelope containing the dress pattern.

Miss Grey studied the cover drawings with a practiced eye. "Yes," she said, "I like that neckline. Are you going to want it in satin?"

"Yes," said Elizabeth. "I've already bought the material. What do you think?" She handed the totebag to the seamstress.

"Yes. Very nice. So you want it just like the picture, then?"

"Well, no. There is one alteration that I'd like." She explained her plan.

"Well, that will make a change, won't it?"

"Can you do it?"

"Well, certainly. I'll just get some measurements. But first, we ought to decide what Jenny's going to wear."

"There are two bridesmaids," said Elizabeth.

"Well, where's the other one?"

"She can't make it to Chandler Grove until the day before the ceremony, but she said to tell you that she's a size nine."

Miss Grey looked doubtful. "Well," she said, "I suppose I can manage."

"Oh, don't worry too much about it," said Elizabeth. "After all, everyone will be looking at me."

Jenny Ramsay smiled sweetly. "Have another cookie, Elizabeth?"

◆   ◆   ◆

WESLEY ROUNTREE MANAGED to get back to the office just as Clay was going off duty. "Is Hill-Bear off on patrol yet?" he asked, checking his desk for messages.

"You just missed him," said Clay, sitting back in his swivel chair. "How'd it go?"

"Well," said Wesley. "I damn near got arrested. How are things with you?"

Without a word, Clay walked over to the apartment-sized refrigerator under the counter and took out a Diet Coke. Solemnly, he popped the tab and handed the can to the sheriff.

"Thanks, Clay. I guess that means you want to go first."

Wesley sipped his drink while Clay explained about his exercise in futility at the records office, and his subsequent trip to the *Scout* offices to read the obituaries. "Actually," he said, "Azzie Todd's memory was pretty good. He only left out a couple of people who died out of the county. Mostly old folks in nursing homes, or who had gone to live with their kids."

"It's a shame, isn't it?" said Wesley sadly. "Not many young people can afford to live around here."

"Yes," said Clay. "But if we let industry come in to create jobs, what would it do to the land?"

"I didn't say I had any answers, Clay. Do you have that list of people who died out of the county?"

Clay handed him a neatly typed list. "I made you a copy."

"Okay. I guess we'll get started on this tomorrow. Thanks, Clay."

The deputy looked embarrassed. "No problem," he muttered. "At least I didn't get arrested."

"Well, neither did I," said Wesley. "But only because nobody was granting Wayne Dupree any wishes today." Between swigs of cola, he explained about finding the body of Jasper Willis, and the subsequent investigation by the minions of the neighboring sheriff's department.

Clay listened in silence. Finally he said, "Did they find out anything?"

"Stabbed in the throat," said Wesley. "The coroner over there thought he might have been approached from behind. Maybe while he was sitting at his desk. They haven't identified the weapon yet, but it wasn't present at the scene. They don't seem to think it was a knife, though. At least not a particularly well sharpened one."

The deputy shuddered. After a moment's pause he said, "Well, it's too bad he was killed before you could question him. That leaves us back where we started."

"He *dead*, Clay. Don't you find that suspicious?"

"Yes, but it doesn't lead us anywhere, and we don't have any proof."

"No, but I have some fascinating bits of speculation. Sheriff Dupree gave me some significant evidence. He said that Willis always wanted to be a travel agent. There were travel posters decorating his office, too."

"So?"

"Couple that with the name of his business, and what do you get?"

Clay Taylor pondered the term *Elijah's Chariot* for a good half minute. "He did tours of the Holy Land?"

"Classical education," said Wesley triumphantly. "I always said there was nothing to beat it. *Your* generation grew up playing with the hamster at the back of the classroom when you should have been studying literature."

"It's from the Bible," said Clay in defense of his grade school.

"Right. And what do you remember about Elijah?"

"Wait a minute. We had him in Sunday school. He was the baldheaded prophet that the little boys made fun of. And so he called some she-bears out of the woods and they ate up forty-two of them."

"That was *Elisha*," snapped Wesley. "And judging from your version of the tale, you must have the Jerry Clower translation of the Gospel."

"I never forgot it," said Clay. "It made me downright scared of preachers. But I can't seem to place Elijah."

"Elijah was the prophet who recruited Elisha. First Book of Kings."

"Oh, yeah," said Clay, concentrating mightily. "Didn't you mention this before? He went to heaven in a chariot of fire."

"Exactly," said Wesley, slapping the desk. "And there's just one more important fact about that little journey of Elijah's. He was the only person in the Bible who went to heaven *without having to die*."

"Elijah's Chariot," murmured Clay, considering the name again. "A fiery departure, but no death. You reckon people figured that out?"

Wesley sent his Coke can spiraling toward the wastebasket. "I bet Emmet did."

"So who killed the provider of this handy little service?"

Wesley Rountree grinned. "Somebody who wouldn't be caught dead, I reckon."

CHAPTER

12

THE WEDDING WAS three days away. Well, four, if you counted today. Elizabeth's reckoning depended entirely upon the subject uppermost in her mind at the moment of calculation. If she was worrying about whether her dress would be finished on time, there were four days left. If she was on the verge of hysterics from sheer panic and overexertion, there were only three days to be endured. Anyhow it was Wednesday, the twenty-eighth of June. In ninety-one hours or so, momentous things would happen. The Princess of Wales would turn twenty-eight, the Fourth of July weekend would get off to a rousing start, and Elizabeth MacPherson would be getting married.

Despite an occasional bout of wedding nerves, she had to admit that things had gone very well indeed, thanks, in large part, to the organizing skill of her aunt Amanda. Elizabeth was convinced that if Aunt Amanda been in charge of the Confederates at the Battle of Atlanta, General Sherman would have had very little time for private study.

With military precision, she had managed to secure the services of an organist and a photographer; commandeered a suitable minister; negotiated with the florist to her own satisfaction; and in a rout reminiscent of the first Battle of Manassas, she had subdued the Earthling catering company—so that in exchange for her guarantee of a generous donation to Greenpeace, they promised to serve both animal flesh and politically incorrect vegetables at the MacPherson–Dawson wedding reception.

Elizabeth had been to a dress fitting the day before and she was very pleased with the look of her wedding gown.

Definitely the tension was beginning to subside, at least as far as the preparations went. Next would come the arrival of all the people from out of town, which would involve a whole new realm of anxiety, along the lines of: what will *my* mother think of *his* mother—and is Daddy going to tell that awful joke about the Scottish minister, the priest, and the rabbi?

The clock on her bedside table read 8:11. Even now the Dawsons would be in flight over the Atlantic, having left Prestwick in the early morning Scottish time (about five hours ago) for their flight to Atlanta. Elizabeth smiled, thinking how wonderful it would be to see Cameron again, especially since they had sworn off phone calls last week as an economy measure. Her own parents had returned from Hawaii on Tuesday, but they were waiting until Thursday to drive down with Bill, who was unable to escape from work any sooner.

She climbed out of bed and put on a T-shirt and jeans, which was all the sartorial effort she could summon upon first getting up. "Now if only I didn't look like a dead rat," she said, peering at herself in the mirror and ruffling her dark hair. "Beauty parlor today."

A discreet tapping at the bedroom door distracted her. "Come in!" called Elizabeth, eyeing her rumpled jeans. "I'm as ready as I'm going to get."

Geoffrey sailed into the room, looking like someone on his way to a regatta. Elizabeth stared at the white cotton sweater and white slacks and then up at

Geoffrey to make sure that it was indeed her cousin who had just entered the room. "You must have been up all night," she declared flatly.

"On the contrary," said Geoffrey, "I find sleep less beguiling when I am busy."

"I don't like the sound of that," muttered Elizabeth. "Just what are you up to?"

"Why, trying to be helpful with the wedding, of course. In order to relieve Mildred of the more mundane cleaning chores so that she can give her full attention to the coming nuptials, I have straightened my own room and I am now gathering the dirty clothes to take downstairs to the laundry room. So far I have mine, and Charles's, which I obtained just now by tiptoeing into his room and collecting it off the floor. He is sleeping like a stoat, so I didn't wake him, but I doubt if he will notice anything amiss. Is there anything you would care to contribute to the basket?"

Elizabeth regarded him with undisguised suspicion. "You're not having a yard sale, are you?"

Geoffrey put his hand over his heart. *"Moi?"*

"I suppose I mustn't be ungrateful about it," she muttered. "Although this is so unlike you that I think you probably ought to have a CAT scan." She gathered up a few items of clothing and placed them on the top of the clothes basket. "Anyway, thank you."

"Not at all," said Geoffrey smoothly. "Virtue is its own reward, in clever little ways." He picked up the basket and turned to go, but, as if struck by an after-thought, he set it down again and said, "Have you heard anything more from the sheriff about the cre-mation case of his?"

Elizabeth yawned. "No, Geoffrey. I told you, I'm not going to get involved in it."

"I found the news of the murder of a crematorium director over in Roan County most interesting."

"It could be a coincidence." She shrugged. "Maybe the business was a cover for a moonshining opera-tion." This was not so much a serious suggestion as a demonstration of her complete indifference to the lure of detection.

"I found it interesting all the same. Thought I might put out a question or two here and there."

Elizabeth frowned. "Geoffrey, if you get yourself killed and spoil my wedding, I'll have you barbecued!"

"I wouldn't dream of inconveniencing you by my death."

"Good. And don't meddle in things, either! Know-ing you, you'll end up getting the minister arrested for murder and the whole wedding will be a sham-bles!"

"Father Ashland is safe from me," Geoffrey prom-ised. "Should I witness him torching an orphanage and dancing naked among the fire hoses, my lips will be sealed."

"Good."

"To further assure you of my benevolence, I wonder if there are any little errands that I can undertake for you today?"

Elizabeth eyed him suspiciously. "Might this end up in my receiving on the day of the wedding a purple wedding cake, or two hundred unhousebroken doves? You're not planning to sabotage my wedding, are you, Geoffrey?" Her voice ended on a plaintive note close to tears.

"I'm not," said Geoffrey, dropping his usual affectations. "Really. I have no pranks in mind at all. I say this to put your mind at rest while I ask you a rather irrelevant question, the answer to which will not, I vow, be used against you."

Elizabeth glared at her cousin. "This had better not be about sex."

"No!" said Geoffrey, sounding quite shocked. "I merely wanted to inquire if you knew what an automobile distributor cap looked like?"

Elizabeth smiled. "Oh, do you know that story about the Queen? During the war when Princess Elizabeth was eighteen, she served as a subaltern in the Auxiliary Territorial Service, and she took a course in ATS vehicle maintenance. You know, how to read maps, drive in convoy, and vehicle service and maintenance."

Geoffrey looked restive. "About the distributor cap—"

"I'm coming to that." Elizabeth was enjoying her story. "When she had finished the course, her father the King went to Camberly on a inspection tour, and the princess was going to show off what she had learned by starting an engine she'd just serviced. But she couldn't get the motor to start! After a few awkward moments, King George admitted to having taken off the distributor cap."

"Hilarious," said Geoffrey gravely.

"I learned about distributor caps so that I could fix the car if any malicious relative ever did that to me." She fixed Geoffrey with a meaningful stare.

"My own motives exactly," said Geoffrey. "You know what pranksters theatre people are. It's just the thing they might do to my car. Do tell me where it is and what it looks like."

Elizabeth thought for a moment. "It's a domelike plastic thing in the middle of the engine with little chimneys on the top or sides and it has wires going out of it to the spark plugs. They're usually held on with spring clips. Cameron taught me that." Her eyes misted again. "Now, please, Geoffrey, assuming that you would have the intelligence to find one in a car, much less remove it, please *don't* do this to us after the wedding!"

"You have my solemn word," said Geoffrey. "I will use the information only for purposes of defense."

"All right," said Elizabeth, wiping her eyes. "In that

case, I guess you can take the final guest list to the caterer. They're making little place cards in calligraphy for the guests. You might check at the florists— see if Lucy's flower orders came through yet. And you could take this zipper to Miss Geneva. I bought the wrong kind and had to get another one."

"It shall be done," Geoffrey promised, looking particularly pleased.

"Good," said Elizabeth. "Then I can spend the day getting my hair done and taking care of about a million other things I should have thought of earlier. Cameron and his mother and brother will be here this evening. We're making it kind of a party dinner. You'll be around for that, won't you?"

Geoffrey considered the possibility. "I have an early-evening appointment, but if dinner is later than seven, I'm sure I can manage."

"Eight-thirty, then," said Elizabeth.

"Yes," said Geoffrey. "I should be through by then."

◆　◆　◆

DEPUTY CLAY TAYLOR felt a little uneasy about going out to question the people at Earthling. He had always found them to be very sincere and committed individuals and he had partaken of many a beans-and-rice potluck in support of their causes in Central

America. He consoled himself with the thought that he was not, in fact, in charge of the interrogation, but merely accompanying a colleague as a guide and observer.

Since the murder of crematorium director Jasper Willis had occurred in Roan County, the task of investigating it fell to Wayne Dupree's organization, but since many of the suspects were in Wesley Rountree's jurisdiction, the two departments had decided to team Clay with an officer from Roan County to carry out the questioning. Meanwhile, Dupree's other deputies were checking the possibility of faked deaths in their own county.

"Though they might not be as likely suspects," Wesley had explained to his fellow sheriff, "because they didn't know about Emmet's reappearance, so they had no reason to become nervous. If you didn't know about Emmet, you'd think you had still gotten away with the scheme."

So far Clay and the Roan deputy had been working together for three days. They were nearly finished with the list of suspects. So far they had turned up nothing suspicious and no one had admitted any knowledge of Emmet Mason's reappearance. Clay would be glad when the partnership was over, because, while Charlie Mundy was an excellent officer as far as Clay could determine, he was also a humorless, narrow-minded pain in the patoot. He was a burly six-footer who looked like the ex-linebacker that he was, and he was a combat veteran from the Marine Corps, all of which may have enabled him to become a first-rate law enforcement officer, but it had done nothing for his somewhat canine personality. It was like going on patrol with a pit bull, Clay had thought—*often* during the last three days. Charlie Mundy had a perpetual squint of suspicion and a crooked smile that he employed when he was least amused. Clay, who managed to combine a career as a peace officer with what he hoped were noble sentiments about the rights of man and the responsibility of the human species to the ecological well-being of the planet, was profoundly uncomfortable in his massive colleague's sneering presence.

"Will you look at this?" Mundy was saying, in his most disdainful tone. He had just pulled into the parking lot of the old gristmill and was presently leaning on the steering wheel, staring malevolently at the Earthling sign above the door. "Earth Shoe people!" He reminded Clay of a shark in a swimming pool.

At the risk of deflecting the attack toward the vicinity of his own soft tissues, Clay ventured a mild defense of the potential suspects. "Actually, Charlie, I know most of them socially. They're very gentle people."

Charlie Mundy sneered. "I don't like cults."

"Actually," murmured Clay, "a cooperative community bears very little resemblance to a cult—"

But Charlie Mundy had already slammed the car door behind him and was slouching toward the door of the herb shop. Clay hurried after him, hoping that he could salvage some of law enforcement's positive image by toning down Mundy's attack.

Rogan Josh met them at the door, looking politely terrified. "May I help you?" he quavered. A glance at Clay indicated that he recognized the deputy, but would not venture to say so.

Charlie Mundy whipped out a notebook. "Name?"

Some minutes later, the entire Earthling contingent had been rounded up and their names had been duly recorded by an ever-more contemptuous Charlie Mundy. His expression suggested that anyone whose name was not a classic English appellation of one syllable was a self-proclaimed eccentric and potential criminal. Considerable time had been taken up in the spelling of the Earthling monikers.

His attitude certainly commanded the full attention of the huddled group, but their cooperation was less apparent. By the time he finally got around to the salient questions, the Earthlings would have denied all knowledge of tofu, much less anything more relevant.

"Christopher Greene?" said Shanti vaguely. "That was Ramachandra, wasn't it?"

A couple of others nodded in agreement.

"Yeah, we had him cremated. He *requested* it," another one offered. "We still have the will, of course."

Charlie Mundy scowled at the assembled suspects. "And he left his money to you?"

They all looked down at the floor. "Oh, money," one of them remarked. "It's of so little consequence."

"Didn't we give it all to the Central American Freedom Fighters?" asked another.

"Or was it the Endangered Wildflower Fund?"

"We want to see financial statements," Charlie informed them. "Tax records. I'll check the courthouse."

"Of course," said R. J.

Clay almost burst out laughing, picturing the courthouse encounter between the snarling Charlie Mundy and the surly Susan Davis. It would either be a match made in heaven (or thereabouts) or a window-rattling dogfight.

Serenely unaware of the encounter that awaited him, Charlie Mundy pursued his next line of inquiry. "Did you know about the case of another local individual, one Emmet Mason, who was supposed to have died five years ago, but who reappeared in California?"

"That's great, man," said Shanti with a hint of mischief in her eyes. "But we're not surprised."

"No?"

"Oh, no. We believe in reincarnation."

◆   ◆   ◆

Wʜᴇɴ ɢᴇᴏꜰꜰʀᴇʏ ᴄʜᴀɴᴅʟᴇʀ appeared at the old gristmill some twenty minutes later, the Earthling community was still assembled, discussing the just-departed officers.

"Now *that* was a major personality disorder, heavily into power and subjugation," said R. J.

"Are you surprised?" asked Shanti. "He probably eats enough red meat to turn himself into a werewolf!"

They stopped talking suddenly when Geoffrey appeared at the shop door, but he could tell that they were disturbed, and he could guess why. "Don't let me interrupt!" he said cheerfully, pretending to have a look at the various plastic tubs of spices. "I know you all must be frightfully upset. Have you thought to make tea? Chamomile, I think."

A young man with rimless glasses and a ponytail shook his head. "Betony."

There was a moment's silence and then a bearded man in overalls said, "You're not a reporter, are you?"

"Ah, no," said Geoffrey gently. "I know as much as they, but I dress better. Actually, you're catering a wedding at my house this Saturday. I have been sent to deliver the final guest list for the calligrapher."

Their expressions suggested that the Dawson–MacPherson wedding, or more probably their recent encounter with Charlie Mundy's soulmate Amanda the Hun, was not a topic they cared to dwell on, but a moon-faced woman in braids took the list from him.

"I, for one, am quite looking forward to your wonderful vegetarian recipes at the reception," said Geoffrey heartily, if untruthfully. Seeing that he had his audience again, he continued: "I am also an old acquaintance of Emmet Mason's." That much was certainly true. Geoffrey had played the Stage Manager to Emmet's Mr. Webb in the Chandler Grove production of *Our Town*.

"So have you heard the latest news about him?" asked Shanti.

"That the initial reports of his death were grossly exaggerated? So I understand. Clarine must be badly hurt by that."

"Absolutely," Shanti agreed. "Her self-esteem is in the low registers and she is letting a lot of negative ionization take place in her brain waves."

Geoffrey took what appeared to be a sympathetic pause, but in fact he was thinking furiously. "I hope you were able to help her," he said at last. "Was she receptive?"

"Sort of. She said she'd start coming to meditation classes and I gave her a crystal to neutralize the unhealthy feelings."

"But it might take a few days to work," said Geoffrey, in a tone suggesting that crystal therapy was his life's work. "When did she come to you?"

"Last Thursday. Her first session is tomorrow."

Geoffrey almost smiled. Thursday. The day before the Willis murder! So they did know. He wondered, though, if they had a motive. The news article about the death of tobacco heir Christopher Greene had not escaped his notice, but framing a question regarding fraud on the part of the group would call for large measures of tact and skill. He was glad that various group members had chosen to argue among themselves as to what methods would best serve Clarine Mason's spiritual ailments. Pretending to listen, he cogitated.

Finally he thought of an angle. "You know," he began, as if divulging a confidence, "call me unorthodox, but, really, the damage to Clarine's feelings is all I see wrong with old Emmet's little deception. I mean, so what if the insurance companies had to pay up? They've soaked it to poor people for years. If someone without close ties did it—or did it with his family's knowledge—I don't see the harm. Especially if the money were going to a cause, instead of for personal gain."

"That's what we thought," said the bearded man. "It sure beats robbing banks to get funding."

"Of course, it could be a bit sticky if the supposed deceased were ever discovered," said Geoffrey, in casual tones stressing the philosophical nature of the discussion.

Shanti smiled. "But if that person should happen to be in the Amazon rain forest teaching agricultural methods to the Yamomano Indians, there would seem to be very little cause for concern."

"Very little cause," said Geoffrey with a nod of thanks. "No more than a cup of betony tea's worth."

◆　◆　◆

CHARLES CHANDLER SHAVED twice that day. He wanted to make sure that he looked his absolute best for the meeting with Snow White that evening. His black hair was newly washed and staying in place for a change, and he had cleaned his fingernails. The choice of clothes was another matter. Strictly speaking, Charles didn't *have* a choice, except his Sunday suit, which fortunately fit him as well as it did in high school. He briefly considered swiping something out of Geoffrey's considerable hoard of finery, but he was a bit larger than his brother and he would look even more ridiculous in a jacket that did not reach his wrists.

What, he wondered, did one *say* to a strange young woman who could not be assumed to be familiar with Bohr's law or the Doppler effect?

Beneath all his personal anxieties, another fear lurked. Suppose this Snow White person had *lied* about her attributes? Three days left. Should he marry her anyway, even if he found her repulsive? Charles decided to postpone a decision on that. The degree of repulsion would have to be measured against the monetary value of the estate.

◆ ◆ ◆

GEOFFREY'S NEXT STOP was the Grey House on Main Street, to deliver the promised zipper to the seamstress. Noting that Miss Geneva's little Buick was in the driveway, Geoffrey parked behind her and hurried up the familiar front steps. He remembered trick-or-treating at this house as a child. The garden was better kept then, he thought sadly, and the paint on the house had been fresher. He supposed that Miss Geneva was having a hard time trying to cope without her efficient elder sister.

At that moment, Miss Geneva drew aside the curtain and peered through the glass panel on the front door. Recognizing him, she flung open the door and ushered him in. "I haven't seen you in ages!" she cried. "I just can't get over how tall you two boys have grown."

Geoffrey made suitable noises in reply. He looked around at the shabby parlor, much in need of an upholsterer.

"Have you brought that zipper I needed for your cousin's dress?" Geoffrey held out the paper bag. Miss

Geneva took it with exclamations of joy at his clev-
erness for remembering, for finding her house, and
so on. Geoffrey decided that Southern belles of her
generation were a lost treasure; women no longer
bothered to lay it on so thick.

"Well, how *are* you, Geoffrey?" she asked, motioning for him to sit down.

"Oh, tolerable," he answered with a lazy smile. "Actually, I came to see how you were. Has someone from
the sheriff's department been by?"

She frowned. "Why, yes. Just a little while ago. One
of them was quite a handsome man—reminded me
of my father. Very forceful way about him. I'm sure
he's an excellent officer."

"They think that fellow Willis was involved in fraud,
you know. Isn't it odd about Emmet Mason?" said
Geoffrey in his most confiding tone.

"Yes, your cousin was telling me about that. How
sad for poor Clarine." She smiled briefly. "There are
some consolations to never having married, and I
found this to be one of them."

Geoffrey nodded. "I'm sure you must miss your
sister, though."

"Aurelia was company for me, of course," Miss Geneva agreed. "But we didn't always get along. She
could be a Tartar in her way, and of course she said
the same about me."

"It's hard for me to think of Miss Aurelia as dead,"

said Geoffrey. "I guess it's because I was away at
school when she passed on, and so I didn't get to the
memorial service. It *was* a memorial service, wasn't
it, rather than a funeral?"

"Oh, yes. She'd always said she wanted to be cremated, so I did as she asked."

"Was the body shipped back to Chandler Grove,
then?"

"No. Directly from the Florida mortuary to Mr.
Willis's establishment. But we had the memorial service here at the church. It would have been such a
long way for people to drive, all the way over there
in Roan County. Even I didn't go for the actual—you
know, the process. I went and collected the ashes the
next day."

Unable to help himself, Geoffrey looked up on the
mantelpiece, but there was no metal urn in evidence.
"And what did you do with her, Miss Geneva?"

The old lady smiled sweetly. "Why, I put her on
the roses, Geoffrey. I think she'd have liked that."

"Well, I must be going now," said Geoffrey, getting
up. "How are the dresses coming along, by the way?"

"I must say I don't like to be so rushed. I should
have been allowed a week per dress. Really, these
modern girls! Marry in haste, you know. But since the
patterns are simple, I believe I will finish them on
Friday evening. Indeed, I must, mustn't I?"

"The sooner the better," said Geoffrey in a tone of some urgency.

◆   ◆   ◆

IN HIS LAW OFFICE Tommy Simmons was working late. It was after six-thirty, and he still had paperwork that had to be finished. When the phone rang, he hoped that it would be an invitation to dinner, because surely no clients would call at this hour. "Hello," he said in his off-duty voice, "Tommy Simmons here."

"Oh, good. I was hoping I'd catch you in," said the voice. "This is Geoffrey Chandler."

Tommy held the phone away from his ear as if he were planning to peer into it. "Where are you calling from?"

"A bar, actually. Look, can you answer me two quick questions?"

Members of your family are always asking me two quick questions, thought Tommy, remembering his grocery-store encounter with Charles. "Yes, Geoffrey, I'll try," he said aloud.

"Good. First of all, have you put things in motion for my cousin Elizabeth to receive the inheritance from Aunt Augusta?"

"Yes," said Tommy cautiously. "The papers are drawn up, but of course, it's not official—"

"And is it a substantial amount?"

"It has increased considerably in recent years. I don't know if you know anything about real estate—"

"Mercifully little," said Geoffrey. "But is it, say, a million?"

"Thereabouts."

"I see. And now to change the subject entirely. Settle a bet for me, would you? Is there a waiting period in Georgia before one can get married?"

"Geoffrey, you wouldn't . . . ?"

"Not for worlds, Tommy. But please answer the question."

"Three days before the license is granted. Your cousin and her fiancé will just make it. I've already spoken to your mother about this."

"Good. Good. What about South Carolina and Florida?"

"Florida is three days. South Carolina—one day before license is granted. I think. I could look it up."

"No, that's okay. It probably doesn't matter. I must go in a moment. To change the subject, Tommy, how is Miss Geneva Grey getting along?"

Tommy couldn't figure out where this conversation was going. "I don't see what—"

"My cousin is thinking of making her a monetary gift," Geoffrey lied.

"Well, I won't say she couldn't use it, Geoffrey. Her parents left a good sum of money, but nobody in that family made a dime after the doctor died, which was some thirty years ago, and they dipped into the capital against all advice to the contrary. I'd say that all that's keeping Miss Geneva going is the life-insurance money from the death of her sister. Would your cousin like me to draw up a deed of gift—"

"That can wait, thanks. Let's get her married first. Got to run, Tom!"

The lawyer was left holding a buzzing phone and wondering what the previous two minutes had been about.

◆　◆　◆

GEOFFREY CHECKED HIS watch. Nearly seven o'clock. He had to be back at the house in an hour, and the bar was getting crowded. He took another sip of Campari, all the while studying the sea of people. Suddenly he noticed the sign that he was looking for: a girl in a white jacket with a rose in her lapel. She was very pretty indeed.

Geoffrey eased his way past several knots of chatting yuppies and appeared at the blonde girl's side. "Good evening," he said softly. "Have I the honor of addressing Snow White?"

The girl's face lit up with recognition. "Aren't you Geoffrey Chandler?" she cried. "I met you at a theatre fund-raiser! I'm—"

"Jenny Ramsay," said Geoffrey nodding. "I never miss a broadcast of the weather. Would you care to sit down?"

As he steered her to a recently vacated booth, Jenny said, "But I thought it was someone named Charles who wrote that letter!" Her eyes narrowed with suspicion. "Is this a joke?"

"It was intended to be a very nasty joke," said Geoffrey. "And the butt of it was to have been my cousin Elizabeth. Let me explain." In a few sentences he outlined Charles's plan to grab the inheritance, judiciously omitting the part in which he searched his brother's room under the pretense of collecting laundry, and discovered the letter from Snow White.

Jenny was stunned. "You mean he wanted me to marry him *tomorrow?*"

"In order to secure the inheritance. I believe so."

"But I'm Elizabeth's maid of honor! I wouldn't do that to her!"

"Charles did not, alas, know the identity of Snow White."

Jenny sighed. "Wasn't that silly? I was just trying to find a way to meet somebody who wouldn't start out being dazzled by my being a celebrity."

"Try dating someone whose opinion of himself is equally high," Geoffrey suggested.

"True," said Jenny thoughtfully. "There is always

Badger." She looked around the bar. "Oh, what if Charles shows up here and finds us?"

"I think not," said Geoffrey. "I have stolen his distributor cap. A little trick I picked up from Queen Elizabeth."

Jenny Ramsay smiled a real smile. "Can I buy you a drink?"

CHAPTER

13

ELIZABETH HAD BEEN pacing by the front windows since before the Dawsons' British Airways flight had touched down in Atlanta. "Where are they?" she fumed. "Shouldn't they be here by now?"

"Not for at least another hour, dear," said Aunt Amanda, who was trying to read. "*Do* stop pacing. Write some thank-you notes."

Elizabeth looked guiltily at the pile of wedding presents on and about the trestle table. "Do you think I ought to write the letters to Cameron's friends as well?"

"Certainly," said Amanda, turning a page. "He deserves at least the public illusion that he has acquired a dutiful wife."

"Well, all right. I think I ought to wait until he gets here to open them, though."

"That still gives you a good many others to write thank-yous for," her aunt pointed out.

Charles Chandler appeared just then, looking well dressed but angry. "Mother, could I borrow your car keys?"

"What is the matter with your car, dear?"

"I don't know! It won't start, and I'm late for an engagement."

Aunt Amanda looked up at her son. "Surely anyone who is a theoretical physicist ought to be able to figure out a simple combustion engine."

Charles reddened. "It isn't the same thing at all, Mother! And I just had it serviced. I don't know what the hell is wrong with it."

Elizabeth kept her eyes carefully turned to the window. "Have you checked the distributor cap, Charles?"

It was nearly an hour later that Dr. Chandler's Lincoln pulled into the driveway, signaling his arrival with discreet beeps of the horn.

"They're here!" cried Elizabeth, abandoning her thank-you note in midword. With a last-minute pat at her newly styled hair, she hurried out the front door to meet the Dawsons.

"How was your flight?" asked Aunt Amanda, when the initial frenzy had died down.

"Quite tedious," said Margaret Dawson. "I expect it will take me ages to get used to the time. My body says it's past midnight."

"Just on eight," Amanda assured her. "We have dinner prepared. I think we shan't bother to wait for Charles and Geoffrey under the circumstances. And after that, we will take you across the street to my sister's."

Margaret Dawson glanced nervously in the direction of the castle. "That is an unusual residence," she ventured. "Cameron keeps telling me that *Dallas* is not at all representational of American life, but really . . . does your sister like it?"

"I believe not," Amanda replied. "It was built by her son, and as you may have noticed she has a For Sale sign in front of it. She says that castles are expensive to maintain, impossible to heat, and very lonely to live in." Remembering that her guest was British, she added kindly, "Of course, I expect it's different for royalty."

"Much worse, I should imagine," said Margaret
Dawson. "When you're royal, you've got whole
crowds of people living there in the castle with you.
Really, out of all that space in the royal palaces, the
Queen has only a tiny apartment in each. She might
as well have a service flat for all the room *she's* got.
And because it's an historic treasure, she can't really
redecorate much, can she?" She looked around approvingly. "I like *your* house."

"Thank you," said Aunt Amanda equably. "I've always fancied it a kingdom of sorts."

Elizabeth, having made Cameron sure of his welcome, had launched into a nonstop account of the
wedding preparations, while Ian asked Dr. Chandler
to show him around the place so that he could stretch
his legs.

They had just reassembled to troop into the dining
room for dinner when Geoffrey appeared. "Don't let
me keep you!" he called, hurrying past them and up
the stairs. "I just need to make a phone call, and then
I'll be right down to join you!"

"Have you seen Charles?" Aunt Amanda called
after him.

"I expect he'll come home soon," said Geoffrey,
disappearing into the stairwell. "He might as well,"
he muttered to himself.

◆　◆　◆

"DON'T YOU HATE THE end of the month?" asked
Wesley Rountree with a mouth full of hamburger.
"This paperwork is about to kill me."

Clay Taylor nodded in sympathy. "They ought to
let us hire some clerks."

"The commissioners wouldn't part with a nickel to
make anybody else's job easier," Wesley grumbled.
"But you notice they did air-condition their cham-
bers."

"Well, I couldn't argue with a thing you've said, but
even paperwork can't depress me tonight," said Clay,
leaning back in his chair with a happy smile. "Because
today was my last day with that Roan County sourpuss
Charlie Mundy."

"Finished questioning our local suspects, did you?"

"That's right. It's going to be all routine scutwork
from here on in—and they are welcome to it. They've
got more manpower than we have, anyhow."

"How are things over in Roan County. Did Mundy
mention it?"

"The coroner thinks Willis was stabbed with scissors; certainly not a knife. And judging from the angle
and the place that the wound was inflicted, he didn't
think it took much force. They don't have any suspects
they like in Roan, though. Word hadn't got out over
there about Emmet Mason's reappearance."

"I think it will be somebody around here," Wesley
agreed. "It surprises me that Wayne is smart enough

to agree with me. But you do think that he found some more faked-death cases over in Roan?"

"At least one person over yonder got scared enough to admit that his dearly departed hadn't gone so far as to die, and there are a couple of other cases that look like people who just ran out on their families, the way Emmet did. I expect most of them had the sense to change their names, though."

"You'd be surprised," said Wesley. "So our theory was correct, then. Jasper Willis was running a travel agency for people who wanted to disappear, and for a fee he'd call up their families with a story about an accident, then send them an urn full of miscellaneous ashes as proof."

"That's what they've been told. I figure that any day now the insurance companies ought to be coming in here like a wolf on the fold."

The phone rang and Wesley reached for it. "Sheriff's office."

Clay went back to his paperwork, but he glanced over at the sheriff from time to time. Wesley had assumed his hunting-dog mode: tense posture, faraway look in his eyes, an expression of complete concentration. The deputy couldn't make out the particulars of the conversation, though. Wesley just kept saying, "Yep," and "Is that right?" and occasionally he'd scribble a few words on his notepad.

After a few minutes of this, Clay noticed that Wesley seemed to relax, and his face spread into a grin. "Well, sir," he said, "I will certainly be mindful of that. And of course we wouldn't want to make an arrest prematurely. How long do you reckon it'll take? Two days? Oh, fine. I'm sure it will take us at least that long to compile the evidence. Meanwhile, we'll keep an eye on things, and don't you meddle in things anymore, either, hear?" He was still grinning when he hung up the phone.

"What was that all about, Wesley?"

"What you might call a tip from a concerned citizen," said Wesley. "I reckon the Roan County boys would have reached the same conclusion, but this saves some time."

"A tip?" said Clay. "You mean about the Willis murder?"

"That's right. Mr. Geoffrey Chandler had a couple of suggestions for us—and one request. First, he thought we should check Miss Geneva Grey's dressmaking scissors for latent bloodstains."

"If she's smart, she's thrown them away."

"He thinks not. She needs them rather urgently just now. And he also recommended that we check the Florida Medical Register for a nurse named Aurelia Grey, or Aurelia anything. He says he'll wager she kept her name, though."

Clay nodded. "That's the old sister who supposedly

died in Florida. We questioned Miss Geneva Grey about that. She was pretty calm."

"Well, she'd just committed murder to keep her secret. Our informant there contends that she and Miss Aurelia arranged the fake death to accomplish two purposes: first, it would get Miss Aurelia out of Chandler Grove so that she could work like she wanted to, and second, it would let Miss Geneva inherit her insurance money so she wouldn't *have* to work."

"Why didn't Aurelia Grey just get a job here?"

"I think they needed more money than that. House upkeep, taxes. I don't know. We'll probably be able to ask her soon. Young Mr. Chandler is pretty sure she'll come back when she hears what her sister has done."

"And what was the request he made?"

The sheriff looked bemused. "He wants us to take two days to complete the investigation before we arrest her. He says she has a wedding dress to finish."

◆　◆　◆

AFTER DINNER AUNT Amanda announced that she would bring coffee into the living room, to which Elizabeth replied that it seemed like an excellent time to open the rest of the wedding presents.

"You might as well," said Aunt Amanda. "The more

thank-you notes you get out of the way before the wedding the better. Especially as you are going abroad."

"And are you going back to Scotland so soon?" Captain Grandfather asked Cameron's mother.

"No," said Margaret Dawson. "Elizabeth has kindly agreed to lend us her car. We are going to do a bit of sight-seeing."

"Perhaps you'd like to go to the Highland games next week?" asked Geoffrey with a straight face.

Ian hooted. "No chance! I want to see Florida."

"I believe I know someone in Florida," said Geoffrey offhandedly. "But I doubt if she'll be there next week."

Charles Chandler, who had slunk in several minutes late for dinner, chose this moment to ask if he could be excused. He said he wasn't feeling well.

"Is anything the matter, dear?" asked Aunt Amanda.

"I think it's a touch of swine flu," said Geoffrey.

They adjourned to the living room, where Elizabeth began to pile the unopened packages on the rug in front of the sofa. "Sit here," she said to Cameron. "You open the gifts and I'll make a note of who sent the package and what it is. For the thank-you notes."

"I hope you're going to write them," said Cameron. "After all, I ground out all those invitations."

"I sent out more than you did!"

"Oh, there's nothing to thank-you notes," said Geoffrey. "Just say *Thanks for the lovely teapot. Of all the teapots we got, yours was our favorite.*"

"No," said Elizabeth. "On no account should you say that. Go on, open something."

One crystal vase, a toaster, and two cookbooks later, Elizabeth said, "Why don't you open the big one from New York? It's awfully heavy, and I've been dying to know what's in it."

"New York?" said Cameron. "I didn't invite anybody in New York. Isn't that one of your lot?"

Elizabeth pointed to the label. "It's addressed to *Dr. Cameron Dawson and Fiancée.* Hardly proper," she sniffed, "but I think it leaves no doubt that the present is from one of *your* friends." Her tone implied that *her* friends had better manners.

"Return address The Package Store, Jamaica, New York; sent UPS. Well, we'll soon see," said Cameron, cutting the twine with his penknife.

Half a minute later, he had cut open the top of the cardboard box and slit one side, so that the box could be folded back to reveal its contents. "Here goes!" said Cameron with a flourish. He peered inside and reeled back at once. *"Bloody hell!"*

"Oh, a garden gnome," said Aunt Amanda politely. "How very British. But that's a very unusual one."

"It certainly is," said Cameron, over Ian's howls of laughter.

"He's quite an old friend," said Margaret Dawson. "I wonder how he got here."

"United Parcel Service," said Geoffrey kindly.

The red-hatted garden gnome was wearing sunglasses and his face was painted with a bronze suntan. Pinned to his recently acquired Hawaiian shirt was an invitation to Cameron Dawson's wedding.

"Is that your gnome from Edinburgh?" asked Elizabeth.

"The stolen one. Yes. Came over for the wedding." Cameron laughed in spite of himself.

"There's no card saying who it's from. I wonder who sent it?" asked Elizabeth, looking suspiciously at Geoffrey. "It was taken from Edinburgh, so I suppose that lets you off the hook."

"It wasn't I," said Geoffrey.

"Then who did it?"

He shook his head. "Sorry, cousin. I only take murder cases."

CHAPTER

14

ELIZABETH STOOD AT the top of the Chandlers'
oak staircase, clutching her father's arm. Beneath the
veil her dark hair curled about her shoulders, and the
satin dress with the low rounded bodice made her look
like a Renaissance princess. Draped across one shoulder was the red and blue tartan of Clan MacPherson.
In front of her stood two blonde bridesmaids in yellow

dresses, carrying bouquets wrapped with tartan ribbons.

"Don't be nervous!" whispered Jenny Ramsay, tapping her on the shoulder. "Everything will be fine."

"Fine?" hissed Elizabeth, over the strains of the organ music. "Are you *serious*? My wedding dress was delivered by the sheriff!"

"Yes, wasn't it sweet of him? He's staying for the wedding, too, isn't he?"

"You ought to be glad Miss Geneva insisted on finishing it in her cell," said Mary Clare.

"I'll never live it down," moaned Elizabeth. "I'm getting married in a dress made by a murderess."

"I suppose that could count as your something blue," drawled Mary Clare. "Now shut up. They're starting the wedding march."

With great precision, Jenny Ramsay began to march down the stairs in time to the music. She had assumed her Solemn Weather Princess mode, the one she used for religious occasions and forecasts of hurricanes. A murmur of recognition from the crowd signaled her arrival downstairs.

When Mary Clare, the other bridesmaid, had reached the bottom step, Elizabeth nodded to her father and they began to walk down the stairs. Elizabeth, while pretending to keep her eyes focused on nothing, could see her mother, Mrs. Dawson, and Aunt Amanda, all in blue, in the front row, looking gratifyingly misty. And in various places in the audience, she glimpsed Jake Adair, Tommy Simmons (clutching a briefcase full of documents), and Wesley Rountree. The ushers—Bill, Charles, and Geoffrey—were now standing off to the side. Cameron, in a dress suit and his Duke of Edinburgh tie, was standing at the altar beside Ian, looking rather like a prince himself.

Elizabeth looked modestly down at her bouquet. There was a tiny note sticking in among the white roses. As unobtrusively as she could, Elizabeth maneuvered the note out of the arrangement and eased it open. In Geoffrey Chandler's unmistakable handwriting was the advice for the wedding night that Victorian mothers were said to give to their just-married daughters: *Close your eyes and think of England.*

Elizabeth giggled all the way to the altar.

◆　◆　◆

"A FÊTE WORSE THAN death," muttered Cameron as they walked toward the grounds of Holyroodhouse.

"They could have arranged better weather for it," agreed the new Mrs. Dawson, huddling under her umbrella. "At least it isn't a *steady* rain."

"No. We'll have time to dry out a bit between bursts. Have you got the invitation?"

"It's in your coat pocket," said Elizabeth. "I checked three times."

Despite the initial chaos of the hasty preparations, the wedding had proceeded without incident. As soon as the ceremony was over, Tommy Simmons insisted upon meeting with the new Mrs. Dawson in the study so that the papers pertaining to the inheritance could be signed. He would not hear of her having so much as a sip of punch before the matter was attended to. In fact, his attitude on the matter was rather ominous. Fortunately these suspicions proved unfounded, despite Elizabeth's attitude of gloom upon leaving the conference. She later explained to Cameron her original impression that inheriting one million dollars ought actually to make one richer, whereas Tommy Simmons seemed to feel that the money was simply a theoretical Monopoly set that existed for the benefit of lawyers. Apparently, although she was rich, she did not in fact have any more money. It was tied up in real estate that it would not be advisable to sell; it was owed to the government in inheritance taxes; or it was soundly invested by the attorneys and ought to remain where it was—for tax purposes. It was a sobering feeling, she said, to learn that one had inherited a collection of attorneys rather than an endless supply of cash.

Other than that, all went well for the newlyweds. At the reception, Charles Chandler took a liking to anthropologist Mary Clare Gitlin. After they had both overindulged in champagne, Charles was heard sev-

eral times to say to her: "If only I'd met you sooner!"
And many of the local guests took home a delightful
souvenir, a paper wedding napkin bearing the autograph of the Channel Four Weather Princess.

The Dawson newlyweds had arrived in Edinburgh
on Tuesday morning, where they had enjoyed having
the house to themselves, except for one indignant Siamese cat, who insisted on being held at every possible
moment to compensate for his week's abandonment.
Apparently, Dr. Grant, who had fed him diligently
twice a day, had neglected to provide the proper sub-
servience that Traveller considered his due.

Two days of relaxation followed—sightseeing and
recuperating from the flight and the wedding ordeal.
The sixth of July had dawned gray and unappealing,
but nevertheless a glorious day for Elizabeth, who insisted upon singing "God Save the Queen" to Her
Majesty in absentia over breakfast. She spent much
of the rest of the day getting ready for the Royal Garden Party.

Shortly before three the Dawsons drove to the palace of Holyroodhouse, with a little placard in the window of the Micra proclaiming them to be official
guests for the occasion. There they joined the crowd
of other distinguished guests, all beetling toward the
entrance to the grounds. The men were in morning
coats or military uniforms, while the women, in flow-

ery silk dresses, strove to appear summery despite the weather.

"Do I look all right?" asked Elizabeth, pulling her white wool shawl more tightly about her. After much shopping along the Royal Mile on the previous afternoon, she had chosen a dark blue dress with a V-neckline and puffed elbow-length sleeves.

"You look fine," Cameron assured her. "Just don't trip!"

"My shoes are all right. It's the hat that takes getting used to," his wife replied, pushing the white straw bonnet firmly back into place. "I'm not used to wearing one."

Several minutes later, they had joined the sea of dignitaries on the palace lawn. In fact, one could hardly *see* the lawn for the dignitaries. They stood in neat rows a few feet apart, creating a path through which the Queen would walk to greet certain selected guests.

Three marquees had been set up to accommodate the guests: the one topped with three gold crowns belonged to the Queen and her entourage; the gold-spike one was the diplomatic tent; and the silver-ball ornaments signified the public marquee, at which the eight thousand guests might be given tea and a cream cake, should they feel sufficiently composed to venture eating.

"Where is the Queen?" asked Elizabeth, peering at the royal marquee.

"She doesn't appear until four," Cameron told her. "Shall I attempt to get you some tea?"

"I'll come with you," said Elizabeth, who wanted a closer look at everything.

At the public marquee, uniformed Crawford's waiters, brought in for the occasion, dispensed the refreshments. While Cameron waited in line, Elizabeth strayed a bit for a closer look at the Queen's marquee. There, superb flower arrangements adorned the trestle tables and a magnificent gold tea service stood, attended by pages in black and footmen in scarlet tailcoats. Even in the royal tent, tea would be served buffet style.

"I don't think I could manage to eat with eight thousand people watching me," murmured Elizabeth. "I see why the Princess Margaret calls this a zoo tea."

"I expect they're used to it," murmured Cameron.

As they walked back to find a place in one of the long lines, a tall young man in a morning coat with a tie identical to Cameron's approached them with a smile of recognition.

"Hello, Cameron!" he cried. "How good to see you again!"

"Hello, Adam," Cameron replied, introducing his bride. "I must thank you again for going to all that trouble over my invitation." Turning to Elizabeth, he said, "This is Adam McIver, an old friend of mine from Fettes. It was he who managed to get you in today."

"Think nothing of it," said Adam, smiling at Elizabeth's echoed thanks. "Many congratulations on your wedding. Cameron and I had many good times together. I remember when a gang of us used to meet in the garden at the Dawsons' house to plan our expedition for getting the Duke of Edinburgh Gold Award." He pointed to his tie as an indication that they had succeeded in meeting the fitness and service requirements for receiving the youth award. "Cameron, I think the last time I saw you was here at the palace when we received that award."

"What was Cameron like as a teenager?" asked Elizabeth.

Adam smiled. "A bit shy, I think, and much less good-looking. He always thought *I* was stuffy. But we in the diplomatic corps go in for subtle humor. Well, it's very nice to meet you, Mrs. Dawson. I'm glad you came to Edinburgh for your honeymoon, rather than to some more obvious place for newlyweds, like Ibiza or Rome." His eyes twinkled.

Cameron, catching the reference, looked stern. "We did consider Nome, Alaska," he said carefully. "Tell me, Adam, do you get to do much traveling in government service?"

"Alas, no," said Adam. "But my sister's flatmate is an air hostess. Good to see you again. I really must dash." With that he wormed his way through a knot of people and disappeared from view.

"It really was kind of him to see that I was invited," said Elizabeth. "Should I write him a thank-you note?"

"Only for the wedding present," said Cameron. "I believe he sent us a used gnome."

At precisely four o'clock, the military band struck up the national anthem, and the Queen and various members of the royal family appeared on the steps to the garden.

"She's much smaller than I expected," whispered Elizabeth. "She looks so . . . *human.*"

The Queen, looking like a perfectly ordinary matron in her green straw hat and summer dress, proceeded down the steps, followed by other members of the family.

"Each of the royals takes a row," whispered a tall blonde woman standing next to Elizabeth. "So you'll get quite a good view of whoever comes our way. You've not been selected to meet her, have you?"

"No," said Elizabeth. "You mean she doesn't speak to everybody?" She had spent days trying to think of just the right thing to say to Her Majesty.

"Oh no. Only to a certain few. They'll have been notified in advance and the ushers know to fetch them out of line."

Several minutes later the Queen walked by and stopped to chat with an army officer and his wife, who had been directed to the center of the aisle by an attending usher. Elizabeth later explained that she didn't know what came over her, but that probably it was the Southern bride's royalty fantasies. After having gotten one's own way for weeks on end and been the absolute center of attention, it is difficult to revert immediately to one's usual humble self. Certain of her relatives unkindly remarked that sudden wealth does unfortunate things to some people's personalities.

Anyway, it wasn't *much* of a gaffe, Elizabeth reasoned, because the Queen is an intimidating presence even for diplomats and heads of state. Those invited into her presence may have fantasies about rushing up to her to say hello, but these impulses evaporate entirely when one is actually in proximity to Her Majesty.

But the new Mrs. Dawson felt that the occasion was so momentous that it should not go unmarked. For just an instant as the Queen was finishing her conversation with the military couple, she glanced up at the crowd and straight at Elizabeth. In that split second, flinging a millennium of social protocol to the winds, Elizabeth smiled and waggled her fingers at the Queen in a half wave. Solemnly, Her Majesty nodded in Elizabeth's direction and turned away.

"Isn't it amazing?" whispered Elizabeth after the Queen continued on her way. "It gave me chills just to be within ten feet of her. I suppose I should have curtsied, but I was too flustered to think at all. I wish I could have actually met her. Oh, well," she concluded cheerfully, "I suppose I'll have another chance when you get your knighthood!"

"Not bloody likely," said Cameron Dawson.

ABOUT THE AUTHOR

◆ ◆ ◆

The Windsor Knot is the fifth installment in Sharyn McCrumb's series of novels featuring forensic anthropology student (and amateur detective) Elizabeth MacPherson. Ms. McCrumb's earlier works about Elizabeth, now considered classic comedy-mysteries, are also on the Ballantine list: *Sick of Shadows, Lovely in Her Bones, Highland Laddie Gone,* and *Paying the Piper. Bimbos of the Death Sun,* her 1987 mystery, won an Edgar Award for best paperback original novel of the year. Her nonseries suspense novel, *If Ever I Return, Pretty Peggy-O,* was published to acclaim in 1990. Ms. McCrumb, a resident of Shawsville, Virginia, is also an Agatha Award–winning short-story writer familiar to readers of *Crescent Review, Appalachian Heritage, Central Appalachian Review,* and *Ellery Queen's Mystery Magazine.* Her other short fiction has appeared in the anthologies *Mr. President, Private Eye; Mummy Stories;* and *Mistletoe Mysteries.*